Jade

Rare Gems Series Book 3

By

KATHI S. BARTON

WCP

World Castle Publishing, LLC
Pensacola, Florida

Copyright © Kathi S. Barton 2014
Print ISBN: 9781629890968
eBook ISBN: 9781629890975
First Edition World Castle Publishing, LLC, May 2, 2014
http://www.worldcastlepublishing.com

Licensing Notes

Cover: Karen Fuller
Editor: Eric Johnston
Editor: Maxine Bringenberg

Chapter 1

"Thanks for the ride. I really appreciate it, Allen." Jade looked around the nice car with envy. "I have a lead on a nice one, and he's supposed to call me back today."

"It's no problem, sweetie. I was going into town anyway. But I wish you'd talk to Blair. He'd help you buy a car if you simply asked him."

She knew he would. For that matter, he'd more than likely give her one if she asked him to, but she wasn't going to. She was determined to make it on her own, and if that meant buying a car that was twenty-six years old until she could get something better, then so be it. But it was going to have to be sooner rather than later. Sapphire was starting to make noises about simply buying her a car and lending her the money to pay off the large debt she'd suddenly found herself in.

A long ago boyfriend had used all her information to open an account as well as obtain a few credit cards. The account at the bank had been easy enough to get taken care of, but not so much the cards. Even proving that she'd lived in this area for longer than the account had been opened wasn't enough. Their logic had been that she could have opened the account from anywhere. And this guy was more than likely doing it because he hated that she'd left him.

"How's the job hunting going?" She looked at him, wondering how he'd found out she'd been looking, but he answered her before she could ask. "Emerald said you were looking for something a good deal more full time. She told me that the flower shop you worked at is being sold."

"Margo sold it last week, and the new owners are going to make some changes. I just don't want to be out of a job when he decides to bring in some of his own workers. I love working there, but…." She really did, too. And Margo Noel, the previous owner, felt badly about it. "The forestry service isn't looking for full-time help right now either. My boss there said it would be well into next year before they had the funding for that, too. I'm not having a great deal of luck anyway."

"Times are tough. Blair was telling me that most of the kids coming out of college right now are having a hard time finding work. Some of them have degrees in computers, too." She nodded, knowing that what he was saying was right. "Annabelle said that your sister is going to work at that new school or she might be out of work, too."

Emerald had signed on to work at the paranormal school that Blair had set up. She'd been set to work at a regular school, but that had fallen through because of funding. Too bad for the other teachers, but great for her sister.

"I have an interview with a firm in the city. It would mean moving there, but I have to do something." Allen nodded. "There are days when I just wish I'd stayed back home and not moved with the family."

Jade turned away, not wanting Allen to see her tears. Lately it had been like that for her. She'd cry at everything. Knowing that her sisters were happy was great, but Jade was really depressed that things just didn't seem to be going her way.

She got out of the car after thanking Allen again for the ride. He told her he'd see her after work if she'd call him, but she had planned on staying at a cheap hotel just so no one would have to come and get her, as well as to be alone for a while. She thought she needed that more than anything…a place to get away and get her head on straight.

"You call me when you're done." She nodded, knowing that she wouldn't, but he nodded to something behind her. "Well lookee there. Somebody is showing off, if I don't miss my bet."

She looked at the large Hummer that sat in the front of the Green Touch where she worked. It did look like it cost a small fortune, but she ignored it. Probably some dick that had pissed off his wife and was there to make amends with a dozen or so roses. Jade went to the back of the greenhouse to toss her things on the table and lock up her bag. She overheard one of the women who worked the register saying that someone was missing. Jade went to her station to start planting the flowers that would be up in the fall.

People came and went as she was putting the dirt she'd brought out to work with into the small trays. She was planting fall cabbage now, and later if she had time, she'd get a good start on the other flowers that were on her list. There wasn't a great deal of call for plants that time of the year, but she had to get what they might use in now or they would never be up in time.

Jade heard her before she saw her. The small mewling sound had her thinking it was a cat for a bit, but after the second time, she turned slowly to look. There, behind the pallet where she'd been working, sat a little girl of about seven or so. When Jade moved to where she could get a better look at her, she realized that the child was afraid.

"Hello." The girl cringed in the corner more. "Are you lost? I think there are people looking for you. Don't you want them to find you?"

She shook her head hard but didn't move out. Turning around completely on the chair she was working on, Jade looked at her. There was something about her that made Jade think of a wounded animal. When someone came into the area she was working in, Jade moved so that the person couldn't see the child. The woman standing there looked pissed.

"Have you seen a kid here? She has on these nasty jeans that are too small for her and a tee-shirt I wouldn't be caught dead in. I've been looking for her for over an hour, and her father is getting really upset." Jade didn't say anything. "I swear to you she runs off just to make me look bad in front of her father. Why the hell she won't just listen to me is annoying as hell. She should be locked up."

"Locked up? Like an animal?" The woman flopped down, then stood quickly. After she straightened her clothing a little, she sat down like she was perched on a limb and might fall. Jade took an immediate dislike to her.

"Of course not like an animal. She wouldn't have to pee on a newspaper or anything. What I meant was she should be sent away to a girl's school, like I'd been. She could learn to have some manners, not...well, she doesn't have any." There was a man coming toward them then, and Jade watched the transformation in the woman go from pissed off to visibly upset in seconds. Jade watched the man stride toward them.

He moved like he was on a mission, and when he got there things had better be the way he wanted them or hell was going to be paid. When he stood near her, she could smell his cologne and wondered how much he'd paid for it. But the woman's sob made her glance back at her.

"I can't find her. I just don't know where the poor thing is. I've looked and looked and…oh darling, you don't think anything has happened to her, do you?" He handed her his handkerchief, and she sobbed into it. A small giggle behind her made her think that the girl was hiding for a good reason.

"She's here somewhere and when she comes out, she won't have any idea what sort of trouble she's caused." Jade didn't agree with him but let him go on comforting the woman. "You should have held her hand and not let her go. I know she likes to run, but I didn't want her to get out where she could do anything to any of the plants."

Jade turned back to her work, ignoring the couple and wishing they'd simply go away. The man was great looking, yes, but not her type. She went more for the kind of man that hit you once or twice when you didn't have what he wanted, then would steal what he thought might bring him a buck or two. That wasn't really true, but it seemed to be the type of man she attracted. The past two men in her life had been abusers, and she had decided that it really wasn't worth trying to find her mate if all she got was duds. Jade looked up when the man touched her shoulder.

"You really are into your work, aren't you?" Jade saw that the woman was glaring at her, and Jade decided that these two suited each other. "I was wondering if you saw my daughter. She's about four foot nine and a little on the thin side. She has dark hair and is wearing a pair of blue jeans and a green tee. Her name is Angie. We came in here to have a look around before tomorrow and now…now she's run off."

"I might have." Jade started to tell him where she was when the other woman spoke up. This was going to be a problem, Jade just knew it.

"When I asked you where she was, you said you didn't know. You said that...you told me that you wouldn't help me." Jade raised a brow at her, but she seemed to be on a roll. "In fact, all you asked me about was if she was a rich man's kid."

"You're a liar." Jade stood up and towered over the woman. The man moved back, but Jade saw that he didn't move to protect the other woman. As Jade moved around the pallet, the woman cringed away from her.

"You touch me and I'll own you." The words rang in the air between them, and Jade took a step back. She wasn't afraid of the woman, but she didn't want to hurt her. She took another step back as the man moved to just beside her.

"Angie, where have you been hiding?" Jade didn't take her eyes off the woman in front of her as Angie moved toward her father. "Come on, honey, you've caused enough problems today."

"She hurt me, Daddy. I don't like her." The man looked at the woman but didn't say anything as he held the little girl. "I want her gone. She hurt me again and I hate her."

Jade moved around the three of them and toward the back where her things were. There was no way she was going to stand there and take this kind of crap from anyone. She found Margo in the office talking to a man in a suit. When she looked at her, Jade knew that something had happened.

"The new owner is here. He and his girlfriend are trying to find his little girl." She sniffled a little, and Jade had an overwhelming urge to join her. "This is his accountant and brother. He's going over the books."

If anyone should be crying, Jade thought it should be the accountant. Jade had seen Margo's books, and they were a nightmare to say the least. And her filing system pretty much consisted of her stuffing things in a shoebox and never looking at them again. Which she was pretty sure had happened.

"I think I met them."

She was suddenly pushed forward hard from behind and fell into the wall. When she turned, the other woman was standing there and she didn't look happy. Jade tried to calm her wolf, but she wanted blood.

"You fucking cunt. You knew where she was all the time and you waited to tell him so that I'd look bad. Well, I got news for you. He's going to marry me, not some little nobody like you. And when he does, I'm going to have this place bulldozed with you in it." Jade looked at her hand and didn't see a ring. That seemed to piss her off more. "He'll marry me, you wait and see."

"Why marry the cow when the milk is free?" The words slipped from her mouth before she could think about them. The woman leapt at her just as the accountant moved forward. Before Jade could react or do anything, the man stepped between the two of them. And Jade's wolf snarled at the new wolf in front of her.

~~~

Quentin's head was pounding. All he'd wanted to do was stop by and see the place before heading to the hotel to meet up with his friend Thad. And now Debra was pissed off, Angie was crying, and the woman he'd bought the place from was crying. Then there was the beautiful woman who had somehow managed to hit Debra, or so she'd said. Margo had called her Jade.

"You should have heard her. She called me a cow." Debra sobbed again into the paper towel that he'd handed her. "Then as I walked into here, she attacked me physically."

Quentin looked at his brother Roger, then at Margo. Neither of them had said anything since he'd walked in. The woman in the corner hadn't either, but Christ, she was pissed off. And for some reason Quentin thought it made her look lovelier.

"Did you see what happened?" Roger looked at Debra when he asked him. "Who attacked who?"

"Quentin, you're not saying you believe that bitch over me, are you?"

Quentin didn't answer Debra as he waited for Roger to answer. "If you saw something different, let me know."

"Debra has the right of it." The girl in the corner growled low. It took Quentin a few seconds to realize she was what his brother was, a wolf. When she started to pace, he realized that she moved like one, sleek and very aware of her body. When she turned to look at him, Quentin suddenly imagined fucking her.

"Margo, what happened here?" The older woman looked at him, then at Jade. Before he could ask her again, Margo spoke.

"She's telling the truth. I...Jade was in the wrong." A lie and every one of them knew it. But he'd asked and now that he'd had an answer, although not the real one, he had to do something.

"Forget it. I so don't need this shit." Jade moved to the office behind her and was out again before he could ask where she was going. He started to follow her when Debra stepped in front of him.

"Let her go. You were going to have to fire them all anyway, right? What do you care if one of them quits? It's less unemployment you have to pay out." Quentin looked at her, then at the other two in the room. Had he not had an audience, he might have told her to fuck off. The woman had been driving him nuts for three weeks now, and he was going to have to end it.

"I can't have her destroying the place before she leaves, can I?" She moved out of his way but followed him. By the time he figured out where she might have gone, Jade was gone. He went to the front of the shop again to see a cab pulling away. He got the number and went back inside. He asked Margo to show him around the place and asked Debra to wait for him.

"She didn't touch that woman." Quentin had thought he'd have to threaten her for answers, but she blurted it out as soon as they were away from the tiny office. "Jade's a good girl, and I did her wrong because…well, because I thought it would save me a job, but I can't do that to her. She's a good girl and don't deserve me lying on her like I did."

"So Debra hit her." She nodded. "And Jade, I'm assuming she didn't retaliate like Debra claimed."

"No, she didn't hurt her none. You could tell she wanted to, but she didn't. Now she's going to hate me and I didn't do nothing to stop her." He told her it would be all right, he'd make it right for her. "I don't think you can. She was going to take that job in the city, and I'm thinking she'll be moving soon. Her family will be upset. They're real close, you see."

Quentin didn't, but that wasn't anything new. He loved his daughter to death, but she was all he had, all he wanted. Then he realized that Margo was still talking; he tried to cut her off when he realized what she'd said.

"What do you mean Jade is already depressed? You think she might try to hurt herself?" The older woman shrugged. "Where does she live?"

Christ, all he needed was one of his employees killing themselves over Debra. He moved to the back of the office to find his daughter when he remembered Debra. He thought about how to get her to go back to the hotel when Roger spoke.

"I'm going to find me a place to stay tonight and then have some drinks. Do you think it would be okay if I didn't have dinner with you guys tonight?" He looked at Debra, who was smiling at him as if she knew something wonderful.

"That's fine. I just heard from Thad, and he wants me to meet him at his house and meet his family. I think he has like, five kids." Not true, of course, but maybe Debra wouldn't want to go if she thought children were involved. "What do you think, Debra? Want to go and meet my new business partner?"

"I've had enough excitement for one day. Would you mind terribly if I went with Roger back to the hotel? I'm exhausted and want to turn in early." She smiled at him, her teeth barely showing through her lips. He thought of Jade's mouth and wondered how she looked when she smiled. Shaking his head, he asked Angie if she wanted to go with him. She, of course, jumped at the chance.

They were on the highway to the address he'd punched into his phone's GPS when he looked at his daughter in the back seat. He couldn't let her go to this house expecting a bunch of kids and being disappointed. He glanced at her in the mirror before speaking.

"I'm not going to Thad's house, baby. We're going to Jade's house." She looked at him with a grin. "I don't know if she has children or not, but I told a fib to Debra."

"So she wouldn't want to go with us." He tried to hide his laughter, but he was pretty sure she'd heard him. "I don't like her. She's mean to everybody, and she only wants to be with me on account of you having a nice bank. Why does she care if you have a piggy bank or not?"

"Did you hear her say that?" Angie nodded. "I see. I think she wants Daddy to marry her, and I'm not going to do that. I have enough going on in my life right now without Debra as my wife."

Angie laughed, and he joined her. Leave it to a child to see right to the heart of things. When he pulled in front of the large house, he thought of all the things he'd do with something this big, and decided that he was going to have to find him and Angie a house soon. Living out of a hotel wasn't fun for a six-year-old.

The woman who was sitting on the porch waved at them as he got Angie out of the car. When she came forward, Quentin thought she was lovely and decided that he'd love to have a woman like this as a grandmother of his child, and not one like his own mom. The woman smiled at him.

"You're either lost or you was looking for one of my granddaughters. There are only two here now, but they'll be home for dinner around six. Which one you looking for?"

"Jade? Does a Jade live here?" She nodded at him and frowned. "I'm sorry, I'm Quentin Witt, and this is my daughter Angie. We just bought the Green Touch. There was a misunderstanding at the shop today, and I believe your granddaughter might have been hurt by it."

"Hurt or pissed off?" He felt his body tense at the sound of the male voice behind him. The man sounded like he was a little pissed himself. Quentin turned. "Hurt or did you piss her off?"

"Pissed. There was an incident where she was wrongly accused and then Margo, the previous owner, said that Jade had been depressed lately and I wanted to make sure she was all right." The man looked over his shoulder, and Quentin turned. He felt as if he'd walked in on a fashion shoot and the models were all there before him.

"My wife said she's not here." Quentin turned back to the man. "You can wait, but if you pissed her off, Jade might be out where she won't come home until she's cooled off. And she won't come here at all if she knows you're here."

"I'm staying in town at the bed and breakfast on Taylor. I would like to speak to her if possible." The man nodded. "I'm supposed to meet a friend of mine for dinner. Perhaps you know him…Thad Galloway."

"You're that prissy ass that bought the Green Touch?" The man laughed. "You should come on up to the house then. Thad is married to my sister-in-law, Diamond. I'm Blair Henson, and that lovely woman in the blue blouse is my wife, Sapphire. Welcome to the home of the rare gems."

Chapter 2

Jade sat in the lobby for another forty-five minutes before she went to the desk again. This was just stupid. She'd been here for over two hours for an interview, and the time for it had come and gone and still nobody had come to get her.

"I'm sorry. But do you know if the interviews are still going on? I've been waiting for my ten o'clock appointment for some time." The woman at the desk barely glanced up from the phone she was texting on. Jade had a sudden urge to reach out and take it from her. "Excuse me."

"You missed it." Jade started to point out she'd been thirty minutes early for her appointment, but the woman continued. "He's already hired someone for the job. Yesterday, I think."

"Yesterday? Then why did you allow me to set up this interview this morning?" The girl shrugged, and Jade reached out for the phone. "When someone talks to you, it's polite to look at them. Why did you make this appointment for me to come in to an interview when the job has been filled?"

"I do all kinds of shit like that to people. Get over it." The girl snatched her phone back. "And for the record, Mr. Wright isn't even in today. He's on vacation with his wife. They left this morning."

17

Jade had to count to ten, then to forty before she felt she could speak again. But by then little Miss Texting was back at her "job" and no doubt using stupid words like *lol, omg,* and *ttyl.* She was nearly to the lower floors when she realized that she was still unemployed, and she had to find a way back home before her family came after her.

"Not a good day, huh?" Jade wanted to ignore her sister, Sapphire, when she touched her mind, but knew that it would do little good. *"I'm guessing that now that you've done whatever it is that you felt the need to hide from us, you'll be home tonight."*

"Not unless one of you come and get me, and I'm really in no mood for chit chat. Just leave me alone and I'll be home tomorrow." Sapphire wasn't usually one to take no for an answer, and today was one of those days.

"I've got someone coming to pick you up. And you'll be nice to him. He's Thad's business partner, and we want to play nice with him." She didn't know why she had to play nice with him when she wasn't going to be working for him, but before she could comment, Sapphire continued. *"And when you get here, I expect you to be nice to everyone, too. I mean it, Jade, you've been in this snit long enough. Either tell me what's going on or I'll have to get it some other way."*

Jade stopped walking, and a woman bumped into her from behind. It took Jade a few seconds to realize that the woman had called her a fucking cunt. But she was too busy thinking what her sister would do to find out information to bother with her.

"Why?" When Sapphire didn't answer her, she continued. *"I mean, what do you care if I'm having a shitty life, am unemployed, broke, and have no prospects of getting a better life, a job, or more money? I'm sure you have more important things to do than to be concerned with me and my troubles."*

"Not really." Jade wanted to believe that, but she knew better. *"For your information, you can have a better car if you want it. Money, too, if that's all this is about. As for your job, I've told you numerous times that I'd hire you and pay you well, too. So, I believe, has Blair. As for the better life? You have to want that or it'll never come to you."*

"Says the person who has it all." Sapphire asked her what she'd said, and Jade told her nothing. *"I'll make my own way home. And I'll be nice from my bedroom. I'm in no mood to fuck with anyone else today, and unless you want me to stay here, then you'll agree."*

Jade was packing up her things at the motel when her sister finally answered her. She agreed that she might be better off in her room if she was going to be a bitch.

"I do that so well. And you'll not give me shit about the car or a job. I'm doing this on my own." Sapphire wouldn't agree to that, but Jade didn't care. She'd either leave her alone or she'd move out. It was as simple as that. And if she had to live on the streets, it would be a great deal better than having them look at her with pity. She saw enough of that when she looked in the mirror every day.

Jade started walking toward home. She could have shifted and ran through the woods, but she didn't want to get home any faster than she had to. There was just too much happiness going on there right now.

She didn't begrudge her sisters their happiness. Jade was thrilled to death for them. Sapphire and Blair were so sweet together, and Thad was getting used to being a wolf and made her laugh whenever he came to her or one of the others with a question. Even her other sisters were happy. Ruby was in her last year of her residency before being a full-time doctor, Emerald was doing what she loved more than life, and even Opal was having some pretty good success at selling her art online. Jade was doing nothing.

The cars drove by her without stopping. She supposed that was a good thing. It wasn't like she was going to ride with anyone she didn't know. It was only eight miles from the house to town, and she walked a good deal more than that daily at either job. Especially at the forestry one.

She was a naturalist there, and one that would have more people show up to her walks and talks than any other worker. Mostly she thought because she'd run with most of the animals in the park, and all of them knew her. She had the most bear sightings of any other person who worked there.

The horn startled her out of her musings. She turned to see the large vehicle pacing her, and she waved the driver around her. He beeped his horn again and pulled up across from her. It was the man from the Green Touch.

"You headed home?" She nodded before thinking about how he knew where she was headed. "Come on, Angie and I will give you a lift. We're headed that way, too."

"I can walk." He laughed. "Seriously, I'd rather walk, and I'm sure my house is out of the way. Just be on your way."

"We're headed to your house, Jade." His voice was still full of humor, but there was a hardness to it, like he didn't like that she'd told him no. Well, he'd have to get over it.

"Then you'll tell them I'm on my way." She waved him on. But he stopped his car altogether and got out on his side. Jade heard the little girl laughing from within the car, but was too pissed off to think how cute it was. The man currently stalking toward her had her undivided attention.

"I said I'd walk." He nodded and opened the door near her. "I'm not getting in that thing with you. I don't even like you, much less know you. You're stupider than that cow you sleep with if you think that—"

"Get in the car, or so help me, I'll leave it parked here and my daughter and I will walk the rest of the way with you just to piss you off more." She glared and he didn't even blink. "I'm going to count to ten, then I'm going to—"

"I'm not five. Don't talk to me—"

"Then fucking act like it. Get in the fucking car before I do something you're going to be even more pissed about." Another car drove around them, honking his horn and cursing at them. "You're going to cause an accident if you don't get in. Is that what you want?"

Two more cars drove around them, and she knew that if she didn't get in he was going to do just what he said he'd do. And it was at least another five miles to her house. She jerked the door from him and got in the car. He slammed the door shut and moved to the other side. He had to wait for several minutes before he could get in, as there was a line of cars now trying to get around him.

He didn't speak to her, which was good because she wasn't sure she'd have been able to hold her temper with the little girl in the car. When Angie said her name, she turned to look at her and saw the large scratch on her face.

"Who did that to you?" She had to take several deep breaths before she could speak again, because she knew she'd frightened the little girl. "I'm sorry, honey. Who scratched you?"

"I fell." It was a lie and they both knew it. The only person who didn't seem to know that someone, not something, had hurt his daughter was the man driving. Jade watched the little girl as she squirmed on her seat, but she didn't say anything else. Jade would bet her last buck that Angie's uncle had done it.

As soon as they stopped in front of her house, she jumped out of the car. She might have made it to her room without incident, but Emerald caught her coming in and asked to speak to her. She went to Blair's office with her and shut the door.

"I have to tell you something. I don't want you to freak out or anything, but I applied for you a job." Jade sat down on the chair just behind her. "It's not much, but it's full-time. They needed someone to help out with the building, and I knew you'd lost your job at the Touch so I put your name in."

"How?" Emerald sat down, too. "You just filled out an application for me? Why would you do that?"

"Because you're my sister and I love you." She smiled at her. "It was easy enough. I knew all your background information, and your social security number was easy to get. Grandma gave it to me from your tax returns. I don't know whether you're a shoo-in or not, but it's something, right?"

"Yes. It's something." Jade wanted to find a corner and sob her eyes out, but she knew that wouldn't fix anything. "I'm going to be sued in a few days. The guy I dated a year ago put my information on a loan and a few credit cards and defaulted. I have to come up with over two hundred thousand dollars by the middle of next month or they're going to prosecute me."

"Oh honey, I didn't know. Did you talk to Blair? Maybe he can help you?" She was shaking her head before Emerald finished. "Why not? He'd do it, wouldn't he?"

"I'm sure he would, but I feel stupid enough already without him knowing, too. And you won't tell him either." Emerald was torn, Jade could see that, but she promised her. "Thank you. I'm going up to my room. I'm not in the mood for company tonight."

She was nearly to the door when Emerald said her name. "I'm really sorry, Jade, that this happened to you. If you need to talk or...well anything, just let me know. Okay?"

"Yes, and thank you." She opened the door and saw the little girl going into the kitchen with her dad. "The little girl? Will you do me a favor and see if you can get close enough to her to see if a wolf put those marks on her face?"

"I will. Do you think it's Quentin's brother?" She asked her who Quentin was. "The man who gave you a ride. His name is Quentin Witt. He's a friend of Thad's."

After she left the office, she went to her room. Turning on the taps to the big tub, she decided to have a long bath and relax, then go to bed. She had to work tomorrow and then go job hunting, and she wanted to have one good night's sleep. She was just stripping down when someone knocked on the door.

~~~

Quentin had no idea why he'd volunteered to go up and get Jade from her room. Blair had said he would, but his wife had called for him from the kitchen and Quentin had said he'd do it. He wanted to talk to the girl but didn't know if doing it at her family home was such a good idea. She was a spoiled brat as far as he could see. He was going to simply tell her that he was sorry for forcing her hand in riding with him, and to ask her why she'd been so upset about Angie's cut. But when she opened the door, he lost his entire train of thought.

"Well?" He shook his head, trying to dispel some of the thoughts of her and him together in a big bed when she just stood there. "You're a moron, aren't you?"

"No. I'm very intelligent, as a matter of fact. I came up here to tell you dinner was ready. And though I wouldn't mind you coming down dressed like that, I'm sure your family might." Christ, when she blushed and turned from him, he nearly whimpered. He had no idea why the sight of her in a ratty old robe had made his cock ache to be inside of her. "You don't have to change on my account."

But she did. When she came back out of the bathroom, she had on a pair of baggy sweats and a too big sweatshirt. He wasn't sure if it was better or worse. Her nipples were poking hard at the thick material, and he wanted to beg her to sample them. Quentin tried to get his sexually hazed mind back under control when he realized she was speaking to him.

"...then I was going to bed. And if you wouldn't mind getting the hell out of here, I'll do that." Not a good thing to say, his body was screaming at him. The word *bed* did not help him. "Are you listening to me?"

"I'm trying to. But I'm distracted. What is it about you that makes me want to strip you down to your bare skin and taste every inch of you?" He should have expected the slap, but he was shocked by it. The woman had a hell of a right. And for as much as he wanted to protest, it was well deserved. "Look, I'm sorry. I don't know what it is about you that makes me stupid."

She snorted. "Male genes? Look, Mr. Witt. I'm not really having a good day. You should just stay the hell away from me, and I'll do the same to you. It's better that way."

"For who?" He wasn't sure why he wanted her, but he did. And he'd never wanted a woman as badly as he did her. "I'm sorry. But I did want to offer you back the job you had at the Green Touch. Margo told me that you didn't have anything to do with Debra and her...antics. Margo said you were a good worker and that you did an amazing job."

"You want to give me my old job back?" She looked at him suspiciously. "What's the catch? I'm not able to take a pay cut, and I don't want any sort of perks from you."

He had a feeling she wasn't talking about job perks, and that put his libido into overdrive again. Christ, what was it about this woman? Quentin shook his head when all the while he wanted to explore perks with her. Especially the perky tips of her breasts. He took two steps toward her because he had an overwhelming need to smell her.

"I don't know what's happening with me." She took a step back from him, and he wanted to snarl at her. "Just let me smell you. Please. I have no idea why, but if I don't get to smell your skin, I'm going to go insane."

"Don't. You have no idea what you're doing." She was right about that; he didn't. But that didn't lessen the fact that he wanted to taste her skin. "Stop right there."

He hadn't even been aware that he was still moving toward her until she was backed to the wall. Moving slowly, he cupped his hand around her waist and pulled her body to him. They were groin to groin, hard cock to warm entrance. When she let out a breath, he felt it brush over his mouth, and he knew that he had to taste her. Her nipples seemed to send electrical pulses to the rest of his body until he knew that if he didn't get inside of her soon, he was going to die. Quentin brushed his mouth over hers and heard her sigh. He touched his mouth to hers again, and was suddenly airborne.

"What the fuck do you think you're doing?" Quentin was still trying to catch his breath when Allen started toward him. "You come into this house and rape one of my dearest friends? I'll have you torn limb from—"

"Stop it." Jade was suddenly between him and Allen, and he was glad. He wasn't sure, but he thought the man was going to make good on his promise and kill him. "You have to...just both of you get out. I'm...I have a headache, and neither of you is helping me."

"Honey, he was going to...he had his hands all over...." Allen glared at him when he stood up. Quentin waited for one of them to say something, anything, when Sapphire and Blair came into the room.

"Nothing happened. It was a mistake. I'm sure...I'm betting that Mr. Witt is regretting it as we speak. It was just a simple...could you all just go away, please?" Jade looked at him and he could see her tears. Everything in him wanted to comfort her, but Allen stepped between them again. "I'd very much like to be alone. I've had a shitty day, and I need to take my bath and sleep."

Quentin thought about staying. But it didn't look like he would be able to talk to Jade anyway, as she'd gone into the bathroom and locked the door. Blair stared at him for several minutes after the rest of them left and they stood in the hall outside her room. He wondered what was going through the other man's head when he finally spoke.

"Do you know what she is?" Quentin nodded, then shook his head. "Wolf. Same as the rest of us. The only reason I'm telling you that is because your brother is one and you have to know that."

"I do. He converted about six years ago when a girlfriend thought it would be cool if he was one like her. She was killed three months later by a hunter." Quentin shook his head. "But that's not all she is. There is something...I don't know. I have this overwhelming need to have sex with her."

He looked at Blair when he realized what he'd said. He'd kill a man if he said that about his sister if he had one, but Blair only patted him on the back. As they moved down the hall to the stairs, Blair laughed.

"You're so fucked right now, I'm going to enjoy this. Jade is not like the rest of her sisters. Nope, not at all. She is going to give you a run for your money like you've never seen." Quentin had a feeling he didn't know the half of it. "I think you and I should have a long talk. After dinner, you and Thad and I will retire to the deck, and I'll try to explain things to you."

"I'm not going to like this, am I?" Blair laughed again and told him no. "I didn't think so. I don't suppose this feeling will go away, will it? I mean after we…I don't know, get this out of our system, I don't suppose these feelings will fade."

"I wouldn't count on it. In fact, the more you touch her, the more you're going to want of her. And that, my good man, is going to save you both."

Quentin thought maybe there was no saving him. He hadn't even touched her much, and he already wanted to go back upstairs, break down the door, and take her right on the bathroom floor. He flushed when he realized this was not helping him. Quentin thought that he was well and truly fucked.

Chapter 3

Thad watched his friend and partner. He could almost feel sorry for him if it wasn't for the fact that it was so fucking funny. When he looked at him again, he smiled. Blair was doing a good job explaining things to him, but his mirth was making it difficult not to join him.

"Jade is my mate is what you're saying." Thad nodded, and Quentin shook his head. "That's not possible. I'm not a wolf and she is. I don't even know how that is supposed to work out."

"It did for me." Quentin sat down hard again and stared at him. "I had some major issues when I first found out. You at least have an advantage in that you're aware of us. Diamond almost…I made some major mistakes at first because I didn't want to believe what she was, but now?" Thad shrugged.

"Are you telling me you're a wolf, too?" Thad nodded and waited for him to deny that, too. "You've not always been one, have you? I mean in college, were you a wolf then?"

"No. Diamond changed me. It was the best thing that's ever happened to me. She and I are mates and when she married me last month, we also became husband and wife. I've never been more happy in my entire life."

Quentin was doing pretty well, he thought. The man was in over his head, but he wasn't denying anything and so far hadn't said anything about what he and Jade had been doing in her bedroom. Thad knew the feeling when you were near your mate. There was just no stopping the need to not only touch her, but to mark her as well. He thought about his own mate, and she touched his mind.

"Have you any idea what's going on out here?" He said that he didn't. *"Sapphire wants to invite him to stay here, his daughter is crying because she's afraid that you guys are going to kill her daddy, and Jade is crying, too. I swear to you, a great deal of money had better come out of this deal you're putting together."*

"No deal, love. We're explaining to Quentin what's going to happen now that he's figured out Jade is his mate." He could feel her confusion and continued before she asked him something he didn't have an answer for. *"I don't think he's going to be a fool like I was. He's not unaware of us, but he is a little freaked out about the whole mating thing. I don't think he gets it."*

"Do you think Jade knows?" He told her he was sure of it. *"Then what is he going to do about it? Or her for that matter. Do you think I should talk to her?"*

"I think we should let them do this on their own. I don't know why, but I have a feeling that Jade will bolt if she thinks we are going to force their hand. She's not very...I don't get the feeling from her that she's all that experienced when it comes to nice men. And Quentin is one of the best." Thad knew about the money even though she'd never said anything, and she'd more than likely hurt him if he told her that he was looking for the prick. *"I'm going to tell Quentin about Kent, if that's okay with you."*

"I don't know what he can do that you haven't been doing. Unless you think it will be something he needs to deal with because he's her mate. You men can be really stupid when it comes to us

Erickson women. I don't know why you think we're in need of you taking care of us all the time."

"I took care of you this morning very nicely, didn't I?" He felt her arousal and wanted to find her. *"The way you came in my mouth when I told you to. I can still taste you on my lips. And the way your nipples looked after I took the rings off? Christ, baby, I want to take you out to the woods right now and fuck you until you can't move."*

"Master." She said his name in that breathless way of hers, and he had to shift on his chair or hurt himself. *"I want to please you. Will you let me?"*

He didn't answer her because he was afraid he'd tell her to come to him now and have her suck his cock. Christ, he was hurting. When Blair looked at him, he knew the man was aware of what was going on, but he only nodded and stood up.

"We'll talk more later. Right now, I think your daughter needs you, and I have to see to something with my own mate. I think we should talk more tomorrow." Quentin nodded, but before he left the room, Blair handed him the book Thad had been given not long ago. "This has a great amount of information in it, but don't lose it. It's very important to our families and could get us hurt by others."

Quentin took the book and walked out the door. Thad and Blair watched him gather up his daughter and leave. The man looked like he'd been poleaxed. Thad followed Blair to the kitchen where the women were. Blair pulled Sapphire into his lap. When he sat down, Diamond sat beside him.

"Will she be okay?" Blair nodded at Sapphire. "If he hurts her, I'll kill him. I'm not kidding around either. I just found out that the idiot she was living with before knocked her around a bit before he left her."

"Quentin won't hurt her. He might say the wrong thing, but he'll never raise his fists to her. His dad cured him of that." Thad looked at the others in the room. "Kirk Witt is a sadistic bastard and should have been in prison long ago. But he made his son a man that I respect and admire. Quentin is nothing like him."

"What do you think he'll do about her?" Thad wished he had an answer for Blair, but he didn't. "I don't want her hurt, but I don't see this ending well for him or her. I think it's going to be very volatile until they come together and realize that there is nothing either of them can do but go with it."

Sapphire snorted. "Like either of you did? I'm thinking she'll just murder him in his sleep if he tries to do anything to her that she doesn't want."

"I disagree." Everyone turned to Annabelle. "I think she'll be more terrified of him because he's nice to her than if he were to hurt her. She's not used to men like him, and she'll be waiting for his fists to fly rather than him being a good man. It might be less than you think."

Thad didn't know. The one thing he did know about his friend that he was sure Quentin didn't know was that his brother was sleeping with his girlfriend, and he'd been the one to hurt little Angie. When he figured that out, hell was going to be paid, and he might need Jade to calm him down.

~~~

"The new owner wants us to keep track of what we're planting and any waste that we have. I don't know how he expects us to keep that all straight every day, but he'll probably get bored with it soon enough and we can go back to the way things were before." Jade nodded, knowing that she'd write down every ounce if that's what it took to keep this place running. Vicky had been showing her around the place for the past hour like she'd never been there before. But she was learning what changes Mr. Witt wanted.

Just before lunch she was sitting down to start on the fall plantings when she thought of the man. Christ, he'd had her toes curling when he touched her. She'd wanted nothing more than to tilt her neck and give him what he wanted when Allen had torn him away from her. Jade still felt her heart speed up when she thought of his mouth so close to hers. When someone said her name, it took her several seconds of staring to drag her mind out of what she'd been thinking about.

"I'm sorry, what did you need?" The woman tisked at her. "I was concentrating so hard on what I was doing, I missed what you said."

The woman didn't look like she cared one fig. When she asked Jade where the lettuce was, Jade took her to the herbs where the last of the spring plants were on sale. There was one thing of bibb lettuce left, and a few pots of some black seeded lettuce.

"That's not lettuce." Before Jade could assure her it was, the woman snapped at her. "I want a head of lettuce. Fresh, so I can make a salad for my husband's family. Not whatever that is. Where is that?"

"You mean you want a head of lettuce and not a plant to grow it from?" The woman rolled her eyes, and Jade had to take a deep breath. "We only have plants here, not full-grown vegetables. I can direct you to the nearest health food place if organic is what you're looking for, but I can't help you."

"Can't or won't?" The woman put her hands on her hips as she glared at her, and Jade had to work very hard not to punch her in the nose. "Where is your manager? I'd like to have a word with him on customer service. You are just too ignorant of your job to be out where the public can come to you for questions you have no answers for."

Okay, Jade thought, this could have gone better. Instead of trying to defend herself, she led the woman to the new manager. He was just a young kid, probably no more than twenty, and didn't have a clue what one plant was from the other. She knew because she'd had to help two other customers with items he'd assured them was one thing when it wasn't.

"This woman won't tell me where to find the lettuce." Dick looked at her, then the woman, and Jade could see the panic on his face. "I demand that you fire her."

"Jade?" She wanted to smack him but only came into his office with the woman and told him the same thing she'd told the woman. "You want a head of lettuce? Like the kind you get at the supermarket? We don't have things like that here. We just sell plants."

"And your sign outside said you have fresh vegetable plants. I want a head of lettuce, and I want it now. And it had better not be one of the ones I can get at the local market either. Your sign says fresh, so I want fresh." The woman sat down and glared when neither of them moved. "Well, get to it. I don't have all day. They're going to be at the house at five, and I still have to find a fresh roast."

Jade walked out of the office and moved to her workstation. She almost felt sorry for the butcher. She was going to demand that he kill a cow and cut it up for her on the store floor, she just knew it. When Dick yelled at her, she stopped.

"Aren't you going to take care of her?" Jade looked at his office, where the woman was smiling back at her. "You brought her to my office. Now deal with her. Get her some fresh lettuce."

"I don't have any on me at the moment." She had to catch herself from saying that she couldn't shit him one either.

"You're the manager, you deal with her. I've done all I can do."

"You're refusing to do what I tell you?" Jade opened her mouth and closed it twice before he continued. "You get her a head of fresh lettuce and be quick about it. If there is one thing I learned in college, it was that the customer is always right."

"But she's not right. We don't have that kind of lettuce here in plants, and we certainly don't have a head of it. Tell her to go to the store and get it like everyone else." Dick was shaking his head. "I can't give her what we don't have."

"Then you leave me no choice but to fire you." Jade looked at him, trying to figure out if he was serious or not, when he turned on his heel and walked away from her. She stood there for several more seconds until she heard him telling Vicky to get some fresh lettuce. Jade pulled out the Touch mobile phone and called Blair.

"Do you know how to get in touch with that guy Witt?" He told her he was there. "Tell him that his boss just fired me and he's working on firing Vicky, too. In another ten minutes…never mind, the guy just fired his two employees, and he doesn't know a bean from a tree."

She was waiting on her ride when the big SUV showed up. Jade didn't speak to him when he and Blair moved by her, and when Angie stopped to sit beside her, she tried to get her to go with her dad.

"He's pretty mad. Daddy said that he has more important things to do than to run around finding people who know their job." She giggled. "I think he's mad at Debra, too."

Good for him, Jade thought. He was smarter than she thought. "He's going to be fine. The guy he hired isn't a fit for this job. Like your dad said, he needs someone that knows about this business before he can make it work."

"He should hire you to be the boss. You can be scary when you want to." Jade wasn't sure that was a compliment or not so didn't say anything. "Besides, don't you know the difference between a bean and a tree? I do and I'm only six."

Jade burst out laughing. The little girl was cute, and she was funny. Jade hadn't realized how much she needed a good laugh until then. When Angie went on to explain other differences she knew, Jade thought about the man in the building behind them. She wanted him.

She had a feeling that he wanted her, too, but she knew why, and she was pretty sure he didn't. Having a mate, even one as charming as he seemed to be, wasn't anything she was ready for. Not yet at any rate. The first thing he'd want to do would be to make her quit working, and then he'd pay off all her debt. Then she'd be beholden to him, like an indentured servant. The crunch of gravel had her looking up to see her taxi.

"I have to go. You should go in and find your dad. I don't think he'd want you out here alone anyway." Angie nodded and moved into the building. When she went to the office and opened the door, Jade heard the woman say she wanted her lettuce now and someone had better bring it to her. Jade was laughing as she slipped into the car.

By the time she was at the office of her other job, she was smiling again. Jade wondered what the man would do if she told him that there was a five-day-old head of lettuce in the employee refrigerator that had seen better days. He'd more than likely not find any humor in it.

~~~

Making her way through the deep forest, she stopped when her walkie-talkie went off. She whispered her name, and the person at the other end spoke back to her using the same low voice. Jade had been tracking a bear for the past

36

hour that had gotten into a campsite, and she had to make sure that it wasn't going to get sick.

"There's a man here to see you, a Quentin Witt. He said that he needs to talk to you as soon as possible. I told him where you were, and he wants you to call him back." Jade saw the big bear moving off toward its den. "Do you have a cell phone? He wants to know."

"No, I don't have a phone. I can't afford one. Tell him that…I'm working and I don't have time for him right now." Clare, the dispatcher, laughed. "Ask him what he wants. I have a bear on the run."

The bear stopped moving and turned to her. That's when Jade saw the three cubs. And Jade was between them and their momma. When her walkie went off again, she pressed the button and told Clare, in a voice she hoped didn't carry to the bears.

"Mother and three cubs located. She's not happy with me being between them. I need a team to…shit." Jade dropped the walkie and reached for a stick. She was screaming at the bear to stop when it started running at her. Jade knew that if it reached her at the speed it was going, it was going to be very painful for her. Just as the momma was about five feet from her, the radio squawked again. There was nothing for her to do but try and run.

Jade was walking out of the forest with three other men when she saw Blair. She wondered what he was doing there when she saw Quentin, too. Angie ran to her and wrapped her arms around her legs before she made it to the ambulance.

"Did you really see a bear?" She nodded at Angie. "Wow, I would have been scared to death. Daddy was cussing up a tornado when you said you saw one. Then when you didn't answer him…gosh, he was really scared."

"Of what?" Jade was seated on the back of the ambulance while she was looked over. There was nothing wrong with her other than she'd been knocked on her ass, but they had to make sure. "The bear is fine, and so are her babies. No need to worry."

"It wasn't the bears I was concerned about." Quentin looked like he could have chewed the bear up and spit it out he was so pissed off. "What the hell were you thinking being out there with nothing more than a radio? What if she had attacked you?"

"She did. But it was my fault. I got between her and her cubs." Jade looked at Angie. "You should have seen them. They were tumbling all over each other and playing. They looked like little kids out in the yard. I wish I'd have had a camera. I would have—"

"You most certainly would not have snapped a picture when she was attacking you." Jade looked at Blair, then at Quentin. Blair was backing off, but Quentin was standing close enough that she could smell his expensive cologne again.

"You're fine, Jade. Nasty bump, but that'll teach you to trip over your own feet." She thanked the medic for his time as she stood up. "See your doc if there are any vision problems."

"I will." Jade was headed to the ranger station when she was suddenly jerked around. Quentin was pulling her back to where the ambulance still sat when she pulled from his grasp. "What are you doing? I have a ton of paperwork to fill out and don't have time for social hour with you."

"You could have been killed out there." She shook her head. "I suppose a big bear attacks you daily and you think that you're some invincible woman who can leap tall buildings."

"No, I'm a person who has been trained on how to do my job properly without hurting the wild animals or getting myself killed in the process. Believe it or not, I know what I'm doing. And that bear only attacked because she thought I was going to hurt her babies. When she attacked, it was no different than what you would have done to save Angie." She started away only to be stopped again. "What do you want?"

"You." He scrubbed his hand over his face and glared at her. "Christ, all I can think about is how much I want to throw you over the first hard surface and fuck you until neither of us can move. All night long all I wanted to do was to find you and ask you to show me if your nipples were as dusky pink as I thought they might be, if your skin tastes as good as I want it to."

She took a step away from him, putting her hands behind her back. "I don't know what to tell you. I'm not....You have to learn to live with disappointment just like I have."

"We don't have to." Jade looked around to see if anyone could hear him. "We could have sex once and see if what Blair and Thad told me was true. That we're mates."

Jade felt her skin chill and the hair on her arms dance. He knew that they were mates and thought they could fuck it out of each other. She took another step back. Then another. When she was three feet from him, she turned and went to the ranger's office. Never in her life had she felt more dirty.

Chapter 4

Roger looked over the books again. There was no way he was going to be able to skim anything off the top here if they were barely making the bills. He thought about simply not paying them and keeping the money earmarked for them, but Quentin had all the bills mailed to him, and he paid them before giving him the receipts. The man was getting more and more cautious all the time.

"Where do you want the truck emptied at?" Roger looked at the woman who'd come in to work about an hour ago. "Mr. Witt said you'd have the information."

He looked down at the notes that Quentin had dropped off that morning on his way to his new office. There was something about a truck coming in, but Roger couldn't for the life of him remember what he'd said. Picking up the notes, he scanned them until he found it.

"He said to put it on the left side of the warehouse. There are inventory men coming in at three, and he wants the old put out before the new." Like it would make a difference in sales. "I'll let him know the truck's here."

Quentin answered on the first ring. "Good. I have several interviews set up for tomorrow and the next day. I have an appointment with someone to come in and run the shop for me later today, if she shows. Thanks for helping me out with this."

He assured him it was fine. "There have been several calls from other vendors. They want to know if it's business as usual. I told them just what you said, that they would have to wait to hear from you." What Roger had actually told them was yes, and to double their order, but he didn't think his fine upstanding brother would find the humor in that. "Debra wants you to call her, too. She said that she wanted to know about your dinner plans. She also has some information on boarding schools."

Roger hoped to Christ that she would be able to convince Quentin to send Angie off to school somewhere. Hopefully someplace where there was a pit and she'd fall into it. He hated that kid as much as he did his brother.

"I'll talk to her about it." Quentin was talking to someone else, then came back on the line. "My ten o'clock is here so I'll have to get back to you. Is there anything else?"

He told him no and hung up. Picking up the phone again, he called Debra. Christ, he wanted her to come down to where he was right now and blow him under the desk. She answered a little breathlessly and he felt his cock get hard.

"I've been thinking about you." She purred at him, and he reached down to his cock and stroked it. Roger was hard as stone but wanted more as he teased her with his voice. "I want you to come here now. I've a mind to come deep in your pussy before your date with my brother."

"I wish I could, but I'm in the middle of a hair appointment." He heard the noises in the background and now and then the click of the door before it got quiet. "It's been three days. I need you to fuck me so badly I hurt with need."

This woman was going to cause him so much trouble, but all he could think about when he was with her was fucking her. She was loud when she came, and he wanted to hear her scream out his name again and again. Roger got up to lock the door and pulled the shade down.

"I want you to come for me while I jerk off." She never told him no, and he could hear the moving of her clothes. "Dip those fingers into your pussy for me and lick them clean."

Her moan told him she was doing as he wanted. When he'd freed his cock, he wrapped his fist around himself as he listened to her pant.

"That's it, baby, work that pussy for me. Think of my long tongue fucking you and sucking on that pretty clit. Do you want it? Do you want me to fuck you with my mouth?" She hissed out her answer, and he felt his own climax coming. "I'm going to come over to your room later, and I want to find you lying on the bed ready for me. I want to pull out my cock and jerk off until I'm coming all over you. Then I'm going to fuck you until I come again, shooting my cum deep inside of you."

His climax shot from him. Christ, he came harder just seeing his cum spray onto the desk and floor. When she cried out as well, saying his name over and over, Roger had to pull the phone from his ear or hurt himself. She was speaking when he put the phone to his ear again.

"…honey, you've no idea how much I needed that. Your brother hasn't fucked me in over four weeks, and with you lying low, I'm hurting." He grinned, then realized what she'd said.

"You have to get him to fuck you, darling. Without him doing that, how the hell will you claim you're having his baby? You go into heat in a week and I want to fill you." The plan was foolproof. She'd have his baby and claim it was his rich brother's. Then after a year or so, Debra would divorce him and they'd live pretty on the checks he'd send each month for the upkeep on a brat that wasn't even his. So long as Debra did her part.

"I've done everything but fuck him while he sleeps. And even that is nearly impossible. He keeps his door locked at the hotel, and that damned daughter of his is constantly under foot. You might have to have a little talk with her again." He grinned. "The last time didn't stick apparently."

Roger had told her to go to her room, and when she didn't listen to him, he'd shifted and chased her. The scratch on her face had been an accident, but Christ, he'd gotten off on her screams so many times over the past few days. Not having sex with the kid—he wasn't a pervert—but the screams. He felt his cock wake up just thinking about them again.

"You leave her to me. I'll make sure she's taken care of." He had had some thoughts of kidnapping her and then ransoming her for some quick cash. Maybe he should give that a little more thought. "What have you found out about that woman and her family? Surely you don't still think of her as competition, do you?"

Debra laughed bitterly. "Her? Hardly. She's way too athletic for his tastes, and we both know it. And her being a wolf won't help her either. Stupid cunt just doesn't know when to quit. I'll take care of her today or tomorrow. I've got a plan that will make him see her just like I want him to, just someone out to get his money. Just like me."

Roger hoped so because a great deal laid on her getting him to claim the child. He was sick to death of being broke all the fucking time.

~~~

Quentin watched her squirm in her chair. He had no idea why that turned him on, but it did. There was something about Jade Erickson that had him harder than a rock all the fucking time.

"I've fired the idiot." She'd just told him what had happened yesterday with his manager. "I don't treat my employees that way. And while I generally believe that the customer is always right, that woman was stupid."

She laughed before she spoke. "I guess it takes all kinds. It probably wouldn't hurt you to update that sign. It's getting a little...outdated."

"What else would you do? If you could run it, what other improvements would you do?" She looked at him, then away. He knew she had ideas. Emerald had told him earlier that Jade loved the Touch and had a list a mile long of things she'd do to make it work better. And make money.

"Hire more staff. You can't run that place with just two people and a manager. I guess Margo was trying to cut corners, but at what cost?" He nodded and glanced down at the notes he'd been making and saw that there. "Also, you'd need to put in more inventory. Not just plants, but everything. People want something pretty to decorate with, not just the plants we sell."

That wasn't there. "Like what? You mean pots and stuff? Or more? I'm willing to spend the money if it will help business."

"Pots would be a good start, but...when have you ever gone to a green house or nursery? I mean they sell everything. Garden tools, more than a hoe and shovel that we sell, but hand tools." She flushed. "You probably already know that."

"No. Actually, other than what I needed to make an investment, I don't know anything about a green house. It was a good deal, and Thad told me that it would get a great return on my money once I got the right people in there." He took a deep breath, not wanting to fuck this up. "I'm making a list of people. I've put your name on it."

"I can't run a business." He thought she was wrong but didn't say anything. "I'm just the behind the scenes kind of worker. You know, plant the plants and run the register once in a while."

Too soon, he thought. "In addition to the hand tools, what else? I've been looking online and there are a great number of things that can be bought. One of the larger green houses in Texas is open year round. We wouldn't be able to manage that here, would we?"

"You could if you wanted. There are trees that could be sold at Christmas. Ornaments, too, if you wanted. Then you could close up in January to get ready for spring. People could buy online, too. Something Margo was never willing to do." When she got up to pace, he watched her stride across the room in long easy steps as she talked and walked. "We sell only ornamental cabbage now in the fall. She never wanted to put in any sort of decorations for Halloween or Thanksgiving either, both holidays that would show some sales. There's enough land out in the back that you could plant pumpkins and have a patch for people to pick them. I take some of the kids in the neighborhood to the one in Columbus. It's not all that big, but they have a blast. And face painting, too. Not all the time but at the pumpkin patch. Bales of hay, too. You could make a lot of sales from the farmers around here just letting them sell their own bales."

He was writing as fast as she spoke, naming things to sell at both the latter holidays, like corn stalks and pumpkin decorating kits. "Margo wouldn't even have contests for pumpkin decorations. And I was at a fair once that had people lined up selling things like kettle popcorn and pumpkin butter. We could have weekend activities just before each holiday. Or better yet, a monthly thing to bring in the family that could be centered on the kids."

When she stopped to stare at him, he felt the pen drop from his fingers. She looked surreal standing with the light of the window behind her and her hair down around her shoulders. Quentin wanted to get up and go to her, pull her into his arms and simply hold her. But before he could act on his impulses, she spoke to him softly.

"Did you know that your brother is sleeping with your girlfriend?" He didn't move as she continued. "They are mates, too, if I don't miss my bet. She's about to go into heat soon and when she does, if you have sex with her, she'll have your baby."

"I'm not sleeping with her." He watched her nod. "How do you know that he's sleeping with her?"

He didn't *not* believe her; he just didn't know. Because he'd been thinking that they were just a little too close anyway. Quentin had been trying to work up the courage to break it off with Debra, but knowing that she'd cause a scene had him avoiding her instead.

"He's marked her. And they've bonded, too. I can smell him on her." Quentin leaned back in his chair as she started pacing again. "What do you know about our kind?"

"Nothing much. I have a book that Thad gave me, but I've been sort of distracted too much to read it." He was glad she didn't ask him about why he'd been so distracted, because he would have had to tell her it was her. "Tell me what to look for."

"There is nothing really to see except she'll have a mark on her throat or shoulder. He might have put it somewhere that you couldn't see right away if they're trying to hide the fact that they're mates." She looked at him, then the window. "You can get her pregnant because she's still human. If she were wolf, only her mate could."

"I'm not sleeping with her. I haven't for a few weeks now." He got up and stood beside her but not touching her. "Show me what it means to mark or to be bonded. And how the scent thing works."

She put her hands behind her back, something he'd noticed she did when someone was close to her, like she was afraid to touch anyone. He wondered about that until she started talking. Her voice was low and seductive.

"Marking someone has different levels. I can mark you by simply touching your bare skin. Hugging marks people too if you rub yourself against them. Males will know that a woman has been hugged by another male, whether it's a human or not, by simply sniffing her. Same for a woman, I guess. Female wolves, bitches, will smell when their mates have been touched as well, and can be more vicious about it than a male sometimes. I think it has to do with the need to breed."

He touched his finger along her arm to her elbow, then pulled her hand around to the front of her. She was so incredibly soft. And when she sighed, he looked at her face. Her eyes had darkened.

"How do I mark you so that no other male comes near you?" She shook her head, and he smiled. "I want to kiss you. Will that be enough?"

"It's not smart for you to claim or mark me, Quentin. I'm not…I'm not any good at being…I'm bad in bed." She flushed again. "Not that I'm saying you want to take me to bed, but…"

"But I do. Very much so." He pulled her closer to him and felt her resistance. "Let me finish that kiss, Jade. I want to kiss you so desperately."

His mouth settled over hers gently. She didn't fight him, but he noticed that she didn't touch him either. Quentin had no idea why, but he would bet her last lover had told her she was a bad lover and that's why she didn't touch. He wanted her to touch him in the worst way.

Cupping the back of her head, he tilted her head to give him better access to her mouth. When she opened for him, he moaned and deepened the kiss, tasting her with his tongue. Her answering moan made him want so much more. He lifted his head and looked down at her while he pulled her arms out from behind her and put them on his arms.

"Hold me, Jade. I want to feel you holding me while I kiss you." She shook her head and started to pull away. "I want you to mark me. How will you do that if you don't touch me?"

"Roger will know." He nodded at her. "You don't care? You don't care that he's sleeping with your girlfriend and he'll tell her that I've marked you?"

"No. I really don't. It's you I want." The kiss this time was hungry. He wanted her to feel how much he wanted her and needed her. When her arms slid around his neck, he lifted her up by her ass and rocked into her. Sliding his hands along her thighs, he helped her wrap around him. Christ, nothing had ever felt this good. Moving to his chair, he sat down and pulled her as close to his cock and over him as he could get her.

Her hands worked at his shirt until she had it open. Quentin lifted her blouse up with her bra and saw that not only were her nipples a pretty shade of pink, but they were thick and hard. He suckled the first one into his mouth even as he pulled her blouse over her head. He felt her fingers running through his chest hairs. Then she pinched his nipples.

"Christ, I want you." She nodded and leaned back for him so that her back was touching his desk. "I want to take you right here."

"Please. I want…. Can you hurry?" Picking her up, he laid her over the desk and tore at the zipper on her slacks. When he finally had them open, he pulled them off her so that she lay before him in her panties only. When she apologized, he paused.

"Why are you sorry? Is it because you think I don't want this?" She shook her head. "Then tell me now because once I'm inside of you, I'm not planning to ever stop."

"I'll disappoint you." He looked down at the feast before him and then back at her face. "I'm too…Kent said was I was too needy and that I touched him too much. I can try not to touch you but the need to…I just don't want you to be disappointed in this. And you will be, I'm sure."

Running his hands up her tights to her panties, he tore them from her. She moaned as he continued up her waist to her breasts. Suckling on first one then the other, he nipped at her nipples before moving up to her throat, then to her earlobe. Biting down on it, he tasted her blood. And then he licked the shell of her ear before whispering to her.

"I'm going to find that prick and tear him apart after I tell him how fucking fantastic you were." He sat up and pulled his shirt off the rest of the way, never taking his eyes off hers. "You touch me as much as you need, because I need it as well. I want to feel your warm hands on my flesh."

Quentin opened his trousers and let them fall to the floor. He rubbed his cock through his boxers and then slowly lowered them until they were at his knees. She watched him, licking her lips as he revealed more and more of him. When he was free of them, he fisted his cock and stood over her.

When she sat up, he let her. Her hands moved over his chest again, this time slowly like she was memorizing him. When she leaned in and took his nipple in her mouth and bit him, he rocked into her belly and knew that the moment she took him into her body he was going to come.

Jade's journey led her to his arms, where she kissed the tat he'd gotten in college, to his scar he didn't even remember having. There was a knife wound near his navel that she licked. And when she wrapped her hand around his cock, he threw back his head and moaned.

"I want to taste you." He wanted to beg her to taste him, but only managed a nod at her request. "Could you sit down in the chair so I can?"

He moved back, sitting blindly in his chair. If it hadn't been there, he would have ended up on the floor and not cared. The moment she was on her knees in front of him, she looked up at him.

"I don't know how to do this." She licked his crown and then suckled the pearl of cum on the tip. "Will you show me?"

"If you got any better you'd kill me." He grinned at her when she smiled. "Do what you want baby. I'll let you know when you hurt me."

He was hurting now but wouldn't have stopped her for any amount of money. When she took him into her mouth, it was all he could do not to beg her to finish him. He wasn't kidding either. If she'd had even one more ounce of practice, he would have died a very happy man.

Quentin wanted her. He wanted to come so deep inside of her that she'd scream for him. Pulling her head up off his cock, she looked as dazed as he felt.

"I need you." She kissed his balls, and he felt his cock jerk hard. "Christ, please, I need to be inside of you now. I want to come inside of you." She nodded, standing. He was so close to the edge that he lifted her up and nearly threw her over the desk. Slamming into her almost before she settled, he stilled. It was that or he was coming right now.

"How do I mark you?" She shook her head, and he felt something deep inside of him snarl. "Tell me. I want to mark you as mine."

"Bite me. You have to bite me while you come." He nodded and asked her where. "My throat."

He started moving in her, trying to calm himself. Every time her sheath rippled around him, he knew he wasn't going to last. Licking where she'd told him, he nipped at the pounding pulse and felt his climax race along his cock. He clamped his teeth into her, tasting hot blood just as his body exploded within her. Her scream made him come harder. And when he felt her bite him, too, his world pinpointed, and then he was out.

Chapter 5

Blair looked at Sapphire when Quentin sort of drifted off again. They'd been having this meeting for over an hour and all they'd been able to get finished was a grocery list for the house and plans for a pack meeting. This had all been done between the two of them while Quentin was who knew where.

"Do you think he's thinking he made a mistake in mating with Jade? I'll murder him if he hurts her in any way." Blair glanced at Quentin before answering Sapphire.

"No, what I think he's doing is trying to figure out what the hell he does now. The man looks like he's got the weight of the world on his shoulders." Blair looked up when Thad started pacing again. *"Did you know that he asked Jade to watch his daughter while we had this meeting?"*

"Yes. Did you see the look on her face, too? She looked terrified out of her mind. And I think Angie knew it. That little girl is a lot smarter than I think anyone knows. She's been asking my grandmother how to measure things so she has her fractions right in school. Do they teach fractions in first grade?" Blair told her he didn't know. *"Blair, he's not going to hurt her, is he?"*

"I have to buy a house." They both looked at Quentin when he spoke for the first time since they'd come in. "Do either of you know of a good realtor? I have this list in my head. That's what I've been working on instead of paying attention to our meeting. I'm sorry."

"No worries. A realtor? I know of a couple. But if you're thinking of building, I know where there is some land for sale. Close to your business." Quentin nodded and seemed to go back into himself for a few seconds. When he came back, Blair nodded. He laughed as he spoke. "You are very organized mentally, aren't you?"

"Yes. It's the way…when I was younger, I used to write things out. My dad…he used to take my notes and modify them. Mostly to suit himself, but more and more towards the end he'd move meeting times around and cancel them without my knowing. It's why I don't have anything to do with him anymore." Quentin sat down. "Do either of you know the man that Jade was dating before me?"

"So, you're dating her?" Blair had to laugh when Quentin flushed. "I think you should know that when a wolf takes a mate, as her alphas we're aware of it, too. We can't hear your conversations with her, but we can now communicate with you mentally if you need us."

"Good to know." Quentin leaned back in his chair before he continued. He looked only slightly more relaxed. "I'm going to put her in charge of the greenhouse and shop. I know she can do it. Her ideas about changes were dead on, and she had quite a few that I hadn't thought of. But she…I want to find out what you know about this Kent person."

Blair reached into his top drawer and pulled out a file. He and Sapphire had already talked about giving the file to him, about things that Blair had been able to have a detective find out. They had decided to give the file to Thad, but only if he asked about it; otherwise they were going to do this on their own.

"Kent Ballard. He was her boyfriend/lover for about a year before Sapphire and the rest moved here. He never came with them, but I guess he'd been a tad upset about her leaving him. He didn't have a job to speak of, and Jade was paying for his apartment as well as giving him gas money to go 'job hunting.' You should also know that he's a vampire, which Sapphire told me she didn't know before this." Quentin took the file and opened it as Blair continued. "Annabelle said he was hurting her, but Jade never said anything to the others. And she made her promise that she wouldn't tell anyone either. Otherwise, I would have taken care of him before this."

"He took out several credit cards in her name." Quentin looked up from the file as he held up one of the sheets of paper. "He's charged nearly two hundred thousand in her name. How the hell is that even possible?"

"Jade had great credit before this. She had a nice savings account, which has been wiped out by the credit card companies, and that's not even counting what the bank had. The only reason they're not suing her is because she had to hire a lawyer. We didn't know anything about it until recently when things started to fall apart for her." Sapphire handed Quentin a sheet of paper that she'd had Jade write out for her as she explained what it was. "This is what she is being sued for. Nearly all of it things like hotels rooms, car rentals, and meals that shows he simply partied on her money with women. More than likely they were his meals. When she sold her car, I knew something was wrong and I asked her. By then, she'd been dealing with it for nearly three months. It's only gotten worse."

Quentin looked over the papers in the file, then got up with them and went to the table in the room. He was spreading them out in some order when he turned to them. Blair would not want to be in Ballard's shoes right now.

"Do you know where this bastard is?" Blair told him that they were looking until they figured out he was Jade's mate and stopped.

"It's a male thing, and we didn't want to piss you off." Blair laughed when Quentin nodded. "Are you going to take care of this? If not, I will. She's not just my pack member but my sister. Not necessarily in blood, but just as close."

"I'm calling in a friend of mine to look him up. And so you know, this isn't all he's done to her. She was hurt physically by him but also mentally. He told her…Christ, he made her think she was less than a woman in the bed." Quentin pulled out his cell phone as he continued. "And hell yeah, I'm taking care of this."

Blair was impressed more with the man an hour later. While he waited for his agent to call him back, he made decisions on the advertising he wanted in place, okayed a flyer that Sapphire's company had made for him, as well as put in place a hiring team so that he could focus his energies elsewhere in the business. Blair was just calling in the final version when the agent, a man by the name of Sloan Crane, called back.

"I have a hit on him," he'd said with a great deal of humor in his voice. Quentin had put the man on speaker phone so that in the event he or Sapphire had a question, they could ask him directly. "The man is a real slime ball. He's currently out of my range at the moment, but believe me, I'll find him. What should I do when I locate the IFC? Kill or let you do the honors?"

Blair looked at Quentin when the man seemed to be serious. "Sloan and I have been friends for a long while. I used to…help him on projects when they were out of his daylight scope. And most of the time we came up with our own set of codes to call people. IFC is an Insecure Fuck Clown."

"Yeah, like that time we found that man plowing it to his mistress while he was talking to his wife and kids. Man was a real piece of work. You should have seen old Quentin here when he caught the man—"

"What did you find out about Ballard?" Quentin cut him off. "And no more stories about what we did. Some of it still gives me nightmares." Blair decided he wanted to know some of these stories, and made a mental note to find out Sloan's number. It might turn out to be fun later to tease the billionaire about his younger days.

"He's got himself a new squeeze, and he's been living off her, too. She's currently changing the locks on her house as well as having his things removed. She never gave him access to her accounts, but then neither had this other girl you had me try and find out about. Erickson had done all the right things, too, so I'm guessing this Ballard has some computer skills that got him in. Or more than likely, he raped her mind as well as her body." Blair heard some papers being moved around before Sloan started talking again. "Here it is. He's already been kicked out of his last digs and then the one after that. He's being sued by a bank that he took out a car loan in that had Erickson's name on it. She did the right thing there too. Smart girl, this one. You think she's seeing anyone right now?"

"Stay away from her or else." The threat from Quentin hung in the air for several seconds, but after a little while longer, Sloan laughed.

"No poaching. Got it. But as I was saying, this Erickson girl did the right thing. Showed how the signatures weren't the same and even went so far as to get her a shark of a lawyer. He got that cleared right up for her. Then when he wanted more money to fix the rest, she had to stop him. Apparently Ballard and the lawyer fees have sucked her dry."

"Hire him back in my name, give him whatever he needs, everything you've found, and have him take care of the rest. I'm sending you what I have now." Sapphire cleared her throat before Blair could stop Quentin. Before he turned to her, he hung up. "I'm going to help her."

"She'll be more than a little pissed off if you do this your way." Sapphire leaned back in her chair as she regarded the man. "What would you do if someone, say your father, moved over you to take charge of something? You said yourself that he's pretty much done that to you. How did it make you feel?" Quentin told her it wasn't the same. "Why not?"

"She needs my help, and I didn't need my father's." He looked down at the file that they'd given him. "How is this any different than what you're trying to get me not to do?"

"We didn't act on it yet. And wouldn't have without telling her what we had planned to do before we started." Sapphire glanced at him as she continued to talk to Thad. "I would kick your ass all over the place. Then I'd stop seeing you. It'll be hard on her, but she will do it. You think you're stubborn? Then you've not been paying attention if you think you're any more so than Jade is. She's very private, too."

"So you're saying that I should talk this over with her before I act? Put things on hold until she says it's okay?" Sapphire nodded, but Blair had a feeling it wasn't going to do any good. Quentin's mind was set. "I'll tell her about it. But the faster we move on this before he finds another woman to hurt the better. Even you can see that."

"I can and I'm sure she will as well, but I doubt it will make much of a difference to her in the long run. You're still moving in on things that have nothing at all do to with you." Quentin shook his head, but Sapphire didn't let him speak. "You'll see when she finds out. And you can bet that she will. I won't tell her and I'm sure Blair won't either, but she will. Mark my words."

Blair had a feeling that Quentin had no idea what he was going to be up against. Blair knew these women, all of them, and if there were a more independent group of them, he'd never want to meet them. But Jade was the most stubborn, even more so than his own mate.

"I'll make sure she's kept in the loop. But I'm going to have to move on this. The sooner we get him taken care of, the sooner she'll be happy. And I want her happy." Blair nodded. She might be happy when she found out, but he doubted that very much.

~~~

Jade watched Angie as she ran from one group of children to the next. She was having a good time, it was obvious. But Angie watched the teacher that sat on the bench like she expected him to attack at any moment. When Emerald sat down beside her, she smiled but still watched Quentin's little girl.

"You should see if he'll enroll her in this school. She's fitting right in." Jade nodded at her sister. "I wonder what she sees with Ben. She's watching him like she knows him, but when I asked he said he'd never seen her before."

"I don't know. I was thinking the same thing. It's almost like she expects him to attack her." Jade stood up when Ben did and waited for him to call the other kids in. "What do you know about him?"

"Nothing much as yet. He had four cubs of his own. Two of them are in the higher grades, one is still at home, and the other child is in the group over where Angie is." When he went toward the group of kids, Angie pushed one of the children behind her, seemingly protecting her. "I wonder what's going on."

They both walked to the group in time to hear Angie tell him to stay away. The little girl behind her was crying. And when Ben tried to reach for her, Angie screamed. Jade took off running. Emerald was right behind her.

"She's not letting her pass." Jade looked at Ben, then to Angie as he continued talking. "I have to take the other children in after recess, and this little girl is keeping her from joining the group."

Angie lifted her chin up and glared at her when she knelt down to speak to her. She looked so much like her dad in that moment that Jade wanted to laugh. Instead, she cleared her throat and asked Ben to give her a minute.

"Angie, they have to go in. You promised me when I brought you here you'd be a good girl." She was nodding even before Jade finished speaking. "Then let her pass. She's holding up the class."

"He's hurting her and the other little girls." Jade's skin prickled, and her body felt frozen. "Alexis said he was hurting them in the closet. She said that he hurts them all."

Emerald moved to stand up. She had no idea what her sister was going to do, but Jade reached for Sapphire. She had to know just what was going on even if it turned out to be nothing.

"I'm coming home from the doctor's now and can be there in about ten minutes. Take her into the office and stay there with her. And the other little girl. Like you, I'm not sure what's going on, but I'm not taking any chances. Blair is with me so I'll let him know, but I think Emerald is talking to him." Jade told her she would. "Jade, see if you can get anything else out of her without upsetting her."

Taking over the little office in the front of the school was nerve racking. Every time the phone rang, Angie would jump and the other girl, Alexis, sat and cried softly in the corner. She wasn't a wolf but a panther, but there were no schools in her family as yet so she had ended up here.

"Am I in trouble?" Angie looked ready to cry, and Jade wondered if she should call her dad and realized she had no idea what his number was. "She told me that she hated it here, and I only asked on account that I wanted to go here."

"No, you're not in trouble. Not at all." Jade sat next to her. "What did she say to you? Did she tell you he was only hurting her, or did she say how he was hurting her?"

Jade was afraid of the answer, and when Angie looked nervous, too, she decided to have her wait until someone else came to talk to her about it. But Angie started talking before she could tell her she'd changed her mind.

"He makes them take off their panties and he touches them." Jade felt her blood run cold, then to hot lava. "He touches their private parts, and then he takes pictures of them with him. I asked her if she had to touch him, and she said yes. Daddy said that that's bad."

"It is." Christ, her father had had to talk to her about this? How did one even start a conversation about perverts and kids? "Did he touch you?"

"No. I would have cut his weenie off." Despite the seriousness of the conversation, Jade laughed. "Daddy said he'd hurt whoever touched me and said I was to tell a grown-up when it happened to me or somebody I know."

"Your dad is very smart." Jade told Sapphire what Angie had told her. *"Can you contact Quentin? He'll need to come here, too. He's going to be pissed about this."*

Sapphire told her he was aware and should be there by the time they got there. She told her that they were only about two minutes away. There was a loud noise in the front office and the door slammed open to show that Quentin had made it before they did. And saying he was pissed would be an understatement.

The police were called in, but things went from bad to worse in a matter of seconds. Ben had barricaded the door and held the kids hostage with a gun. Jade had been moved out of the building to one of the police cars along with Angie. Quentin had only said three words to her when he'd gotten there, and those were clipped and harsh. She knew that things were not going to get any better either.

"Quentin is trying to talk to the teacher. I had no idea he could do that, but the police said he's one of the best when it comes to this type of situation." Jade was glad that something was going right and thanked Sapphire for telling her. *"He's trying to get Ben to let the children go and to turn himself in before it gets worse."*

"What if he hurts one of the children? More, I mean…what if he hurts one of them more?" Sapphire said that they were handling it. *"I have to do something. I can't just sit here."*

When Sapphire told her to sit still, Jade got out of the car and stood up. She reached beyond the woods and found three of her buddies. Two were bears and one was a large snake. Emerald had told her that Ben was a wolf like them. She told them what was going on.

"I'm coming out to work with you. Jeremy, I want you to get inside the building from the back and open the door for the rest of us." Jeremy told her he was nearly inside now. Jade worked her way to the back of the building until she found the door that led to the playgrounds.

When the door clicked unlocked, she waited several seconds to make sure that Jeremy shifted back to human. Gilly, one of the bears, had brought his clothes with him and tossed them into the room just before all three went in.

Shifting to their animals, Jade led them down the hall to the room where she knew the teacher was.

All the kids in the room were shifters of some sort, so they'd not be afraid to see them come in. She did worry about what would happen to them if any of them had to kill Ben, but she'd cross that bridge when she came to it. The back door to the room was opened by Jeremy again, and they each slipped inside.

Ben's back was to the room as he stood there. He was at the door that led to the main hall, screaming at the person on the other side to get the fuck out of there. He was saying that he'd just leave when they moved. She knew when Quentin told him he wasn't going anywhere that the negotiations were not going as well as they'd hoped. Especially when Ben threatened to kill a child a minute if he didn't let him go. She told Jeremy to lead the kids out the back.

The last child was moving out the door when Ben turned. He had the gun pointed at her and Gilly before she could blink. And as soon as she saw the look on Ben's face, she knew that he was going to kill himself. Fucking bastard wasn't going to go that easily.

She leapt at him just as he put the gun under his chin. When Gilly growled, Jade knew that someone had opened the door, but it was too late to stop herself. She hit Ben just as the gun went off.

Chapter 6

Quentin was so pissed, he was having a hard time not telling everyone to get the fuck away from him so that he could see to Jade. He wasn't really sure what he was going to do to her, but he knew it wasn't going to be to thank her. She'd nearly gotten herself killed. He glanced up at the officer that had told him she wasn't hurt.

"They're taking her to the clinic." Quentin looked at the ambulance as it pulled away. "She's gotten herself a good-sized knot on her head, and they want to make sure it's nothing serious."

"You told me she wasn't hurt. You assured me that other than her clothes being muddied, she was just fine." Quentin had to stop before the man pressed him into the wall behind him. "You lied to me."

"No, sir, I didn't lie. She got the knot on her head when she tripped over one of the other officers' feet." Quentin asked him who. "No, sir, I'm not going to tell you that either. You'd kill the man before he got a chance to tell you he was sorry. I know about mates, and all you see is red before you see reason. Jade is fine, but they wanted to be sure. She can be on the stubborn side when she's got her panties in a twist over something."

"And what does she have her panties in a twist over? It certainly can't be because she went into a hostage situation without proper backup and nearly got herself killed. She can't be upset because the man she attacked could have hurt one of the others in the room with them. There can be no way that she's mad because she brought my daughter into this." Quentin glared when the man snorted. "You think this is funny?"

"No, no I don't, but as for her bringing your daughter in on this, I'm thinking you might want to talk to the captain. He seems to think your little girl and mate might have saved untold numbers of little girls being hurt by that teacher. In fact, that little kid of yours has all them others talking. Even the ones in the higher grades." The young officer laughed. "That kid of yours...if I didn't know any better, I'd say she was Jade's kid the way she's barking orders around and telling them kids to fess up."

He watched the man walk away, still laughing. Blair was coming out of the room where his daughter was being questioned, and he nearly knocked someone down to get to him. They'd made him step out of the room earlier when he'd been upsetting the other children. Now that he thought about it, Quentin guessed that he had been. He'd been so scared that he'd been a little off his rocker.

"Angie is going to be out in a second, but you have to straighten up." Quentin nearly told him to go to hell when Blair spoke again. "You look in the mirror in the past hour? Your hair is standing on end and you have a glazed look in your eye that's fucking spooky."

Quentin took a deep breath. "If I clean up, will they let me see Angie? I'm about ready to tear the door off the hinges if they don't let me see her."

"I can see that. But you go in there now and they'll shoot you in the head. They're all a little on edge and are just waiting to kill something. Jade took that away from them, and they need something to hurt."

"She could have been killed doing something stupid like that." Blair nodded as he followed him to the bathroom. He might have been a little uncomfortable with that, but he noticed that the police were all standing around with their hands on their guns, and decided that if he had another freak attack like he'd had earlier, Quentin wanted Blair there to calm him down.

"The police are saying that your daughter is a hero. They're keeping her name under wraps because of her being a minor, but she did just what you told her to do." Quentin splashed cold water on his face as Blair continued. "She told the first officer that she'd been told by you that it's bad to have anyone touch them like little Alexis had told her that the teacher had done. You're a smart man for that."

"She was in a daycare center when one of the aides was arrested for molesting one of the children. It was all over the paper for weeks and she wasn't able to go back there. I had to tell her something, and decided that knowing the truth of what happened might save her one of these days." Quentin looked at Blair in the mirror as he told him the rest. "That's one of the reasons we came here. I didn't want her to go through what one of the other kids had gone through when it leaked out what her name was. It was horrible for the little girl."

"I bet." Quentin started for the door and stopped when Blair stood in front of it. "There's something else you should know. I don't know how you feel about it, but here you go. That girlfriend of yours is here. Sapphire just told me. She said she's hanging around right outside this door to see you."

Quentin took a step back from it and laughed when Blair did. "I'm going to have to have a talk with her I guess. She has to know that I'm no longer interested in a relationship with her. Jade told me that...she explained to me that Debra might be Roger's mate."

"I would say she's right. But she's here now, and so are the police. As I'd said earlier, they're a might on edge and could hurt either one of you. I don't care much for the bitch out there, but Jade might get a tad pissy with me if you get hurt. What do you want to do?" Quentin wanted to see his daughter, and then he wanted to see Jade. He looked at Blair.

"I'm going to have to face her again sooner or later. I just wish she'd listened to me when I told her the other day she should go back to Texas. I was going to have a talk with her there." Blair nodded and moved from in front of the door. "I don't suppose I can convince you to shift to a big wolf and scare her off, can I? Just until I can work this out with the police and all."

"Sorry, buddy, but for as much as I like you, I'm not going to stand in front of you when a woman could be pissed. Not only could that woman hurt me, but Sapphire would tear her hair out one follicle at a time if she hurt her poor husband." Blair grinned. "Might be fun to watch, but not today."

When he opened the door after calling Blair a traitor, he saw her before she saw him. She looked like she'd just stepped out of a salon, not a hair out of place and her makeup looked like she'd spent the past hour making sure she looked perfect. Not at all the way Jade had looked when he'd last seen her.

She'd been in the kitchen with her grandmother arguing about something. Her ponytail was all askew, and her pajamas looked like something she'd had since childhood.

There were giant strawberries all over the pants and a little girl with a strawberry on her head on the tee-shirt. When he realized she had no bra on, his cock hardened. Her grandmother made him take a step back when she smiled. Christ, he'd been ready to throw Jade on the counter, not caring at all that his daughter was there, too.

As soon as Debra saw him, the transformation was immediate and profound. She looked as if she was going to sob right then, and her face screwed up into what he could only surmise as pain. He took a step back from her when she nearly leapt in his arms, remembering at the last moment what Jade had told him the other day about being marked.

"Quentin? Are you all right?" She reached for him again, and he dodged her hand. When her face began to change into a grimace, he looked at Blair, who, despite his earlier threat, didn't leave him. "What's going on?"

"I just don't want you to touch me." He'd said it low, but she heard him. "I don't even know why you're down here, Debra. I've asked you time and time again to go back to your home. Why are you still here?" He looked around, then at her again as Blair was called away. "Is it because of Roger?"

Her face took on so many changes that had he not been looking directly at her, he would have missed them. She looked as if she was shocked for a second, no more, and then she was mad. The anger that surged from her had him take a step back, then another. Milliseconds later, she was as serene as though nothing had happened. Her smile, however, was brittle and harsh.

"I don't know what you're talking about. What would…why would you think that Roger held anything for me that I'd stay? I'm in love with you, Quentin. I think I have been my whole life." She took a step toward him, and he took another back. "Quentin?"

She was mad. Not pissed, though he was pretty sure she was that as well. But stark raving mad, mad-as-a-hatter mad. When she smiled again, Quentin felt something move along his mind and he tried to shy away from it, suddenly very afraid. But when Jade spoke, he nearly looked for her.

"I can feel that something's wrong. What is it? Has something happened?" He looked around and saw Blair coming to him, walking very quickly. *"Blair is coming to find you. He's going to help you until I can get there."*

"Don't." He had no idea what the fuck was going on, but her coming to him right now would not be good. Quentin was afraid she'd be hurt. Thinking about how he was speaking to her this way made him think he was a little off, too. *"I'm fine. I can see Blair. He's coming to me now. It's Debra. I think she's lost her mind."*

"If she ever had one." He smiled and sobered when Debra cocked a brow at him. *"You're very confused, aren't you?"*

"You think?" He felt her laughter and relaxed with it. *"She's telling me that she loves me and that she's only still here because of me. I asked her about Roger and she, of course, denied it."*

"She would. He will, too, I would imagine." Quentin moved toward Blair when he was close and walked away with him, leaving Debra standing there alone. He looked up at the man and let go of the breath he'd been holding.

"Jade said that I was to protect your human ass." Blair grinned as he chuckled. "Not in those words, mind you, but she did ask me to make sure you're fine. Are you?"

"I'm not sure." And he wasn't. The only thing he was sure of was the little girl running at him full tilt. When she leapt into his arms, he held her to him. "I'm all right now. Everything is just fine."

~~~

She was stalling. Jade thought her sister knew it too and was laughing at her. When she got up and went to the smallish bathroom again to check the lockers in there, Sapphire finally asked her what the hell she was doing. There wasn't enough room in this hospital room for her to move like she felt she needed to.

"He's pissed off." Sapphire nodded as if she already knew it. "I don't want him to hit me in front of everyone. It would piss Blair off, and he might hurt him."

"Who might hit you? Quentin?" Jade nodded at her sister's question. "You don't seriously think he'd hit you, do you? Christ, Jade, the man is nearly rabid for you. You should have seen him at the school. I thought he was going to tear Blair up when he didn't let him in to see you. And when he found out you'd been hurt again, he nearly tore a cop's head off."

Jade wanted to believe her, but she was too nervous. Men that she dated liked to hit. She wasn't sure what she'd do if he didn't. Smiling, she thought of Quentin tearing into the cop. Sapphire was saying something but Jade didn't pay any attention until she said Debra's name.

"What do you mean she said she's in love with him?" Sapphire took a step back, and Jade realized her wolf was surfacing. "I'm sorry, but do you think he loves her?"

"No, I do not. The man is your mate. And besides, I think she's mated to Roger, Quentin's brother. Did you know that?" Jade nodded but still wasn't entirely sure. "Jade, what is really the matter? It's not just Quentin being upset with you."

"He has a lot of money." Sapphire nodded. "And I don't. Plus, and I know you know about them, there are all those bills that Kent took out for me. He'll not want to be straddled with all those. I suppose you told him about them, too."

"I didn't have to. He said you mentioned Kent's name and he took it from there. He told us when we gave him what we had that he was going to take care of it." Jade wandered around the room again. It was time to go, and she knew it. "Jade?"

"I don't want to start this thing out, whatever it might be, on the wrong foot. I have to tell him everything, and I don't think he's going to be very happy about it." Sapphire sat down in the chair but said nothing. "He's going to think I'm stupid."

"Who's stupid?" Jade turned to the door when Quentin spoke. "Who's stupid? If you think that guy is, you're right, but I have a feeling that's not who you were talking about, is it?"

Sapphire kissed her on the cheek and left them. Quentin looked like he was upset, but not mad like she'd thought he would be. Instead of demanding she tell him anything, he sat down in the chair and waited. Jade wanted to go with her sister but knew this needed to be said.

"I'm in debt. A lot of it. This guy I knew before you, before moving here, found my personal information and used it to get sixteen credit cards and—"

"Nineteen. He got nineteen credit cards with your information. As well as two bank accounts. The second one he applied for was denied. Thankfully you'd contacted a lawyer by then and he was nearly arrested." Jade sat down on the bed as he continued. "Of the nineteen credit cards, only twelve of them are still active. But I'm having that taken care of right now."

"You've been looking into this?" He nodded. "I don't understand, you know about this and you're still here?"

"What he did isn't anything you could have stopped. He was slick. As a matter of fact, you're not the first woman he'd done this to, and you weren't the last. There's a woman in Jasper, Nevada, that is currently going through the same thing." Quentin got up and moved toward her slowly. "I'm willing to give you a freebie on the money and cards because I can see how embarrassing it might have been for you. But then there's today with the teacher. You should have waited until we were able to go in and arrest him. But you didn't. You could have been killed."

"A freebie? What the hell is that supposed to...? You know, I don't care. I was worried that he'd hurt one of the other children. But he was going to kill himself, which I didn't think would help them either." He was standing in front of her when she took a deep breath to continue, but he smelled so good. "I can't think when you're this close."

"I'm thinking that's a good thing." He leaned into her and sniffed her throat, and Jade felt her toes curl in her shoes. "I want you. Right now, I'd like nothing better than to take you to my bed and make love to you."

"I have to go home so I can shift." Her mind was humming, as was her body, and when he nipped at her skin, she moaned. "I don't think we should be doing this here. There are all kinds of people walking up and down the hallway who could come in here."

"We could lock the door." His mouth moved up to her lips, and he suckled her lower one into his mouth and bit her before releasing it. "The bed isn't as big as the one at the motel, but it'll do for now."

He started walking her back all the while touching her, stripping her of her shirt, then her bra. As soon as the bed touched her legs, Quentin lifted her up, and she wrapped around him as he took her to the bed. When he pulled her nipple into his mouth and sucked hard, she moaned loudly and held him to her.

"I forgot the door." Her mind was a haze of need and when he pulled away from her, she whimpered. "Christ, let me take care of the door. Take off your pants now for me and I'll be inside of you as soon as I click the lock."

Quentin pulled his shirt over his head and dropped it on the floor. Toeing off his shoes, he locked the door, then came back to her. His pants were off even before he was halfway to her. She tore off her pants and panties together and watched him walk toward her.

"I wish I had more patience when it came to you." Jade had no idea what he was talking about; her need was clawing at her. "I want to make slow love to you, but I'm thinking we'll be lucky if I don't come as soon as I'm inside of you."

"Please, yes. I want that, too." He grinned at her and lifted her up. When he turned and sat on the bed, she was sitting in front of him. This was an amazing feeling.

"You're going to ride me. And while you do that, I'm going to feast on these lovely breasts." Scooting back on the bed with her on his lap, she adjusted herself so that she was wrapped around him again. When he lifted her up, she was slightly confused until he started to lower her onto his cock. "Christ, baby, that's it."

It took her a few minutes to figure out how to "ride" him. Once she figured it out, she held his shoulders while he lifted first one, then the other breast to his mouth and nipped at her. She felt it all the way to her core and threw back her head in pleasure.

"I need to mark you again. What do you smell like that has me wanting to kill someone?" Jade looked at him through hooded eyes and told him it was a bear. "I need to mark you. Is it always going to be like this? Christ, I'm not going to last."

"When we come, mark me. Make it a scar so that everyone will see it." Quentin groaned and pulled her tighter to him by cupping her ass. "When we come, you have to bite me. Then tear at my skin. It'll have to be hard enough that you draw blood."

He rolled her to her back and settled between her thighs. Holding onto the sheets, forgetting that she could touch him, he growled at her to hold on. As soon as her hands wrapped around his arms, he started pounding into her with hard punches of his cock until she felt it at the back of her throat.

"Come with me. Come now, Jade. Please baby, I'm—" Quentin roared out her name and sank his teeth into her shoulder. Crying out, she licked his shoulder and felt her canines drop. As soon as she came, she sank her teeth into him and growled low. Christ almighty, her head felt as if it was coming off the top.

"*Again*," he commanded her, and her body responded immediately. Jade felt him drop onto her and welcomed his weight even as her body seemed to be still having a climax. Closing her eyes, she thought of the state of the room and smiled. It was a good thing he'd locked the door.

Chapter 7

"The books aren't coming out the way that they should." Roger tried his best to look confused, but he was pretty sure that Quentin knew he was aware of just what he was talking about. "I've had them looked over by three different companies, and all of them tell me the same. You're—"

"Don't say it. If you start throwing around accusations you can't back up, you're going to regret it later." Roger leaned back in the chair of the desk he'd been working at when Quentin had come in over an hour ago. He'd been going on about one thing or another when suddenly he blurted out the statement about the accounting being off by thousands of dollars. He was partly right; they were off, but by much more than he thought.

"I've taken precautions, too. You no longer have access to the accounts as of two days ago. The work you've been doing since then is set up with a dummy account, and the money you've been taking and putting into your account has led me right to your offshore money." Roger sat up now, wondering just how much he'd been able to figure out and who was involved. Quentin didn't move from his position at the door and crossed his arms over his chest.

"And," he asked him when Quentin only stood there. "You've got something you're holding off telling me. What the fuck is it?"

"If you wanted more money, why didn't you ask me? I mean, why steal what I would have given you freely?" Roger only stared at him, thinking there was no way he was this naive. "You didn't really think I'd not find out, did you?"

"No. Actually, I thought with your head so far up your ass with Debra that I'd be able to rob you blind and be gone before you figured it out." Roger stood up, picking up the single key off the desk and slipping it into his pocket as he started pacing the room. "I thought for sure that you'd be married by now, too, but I can see…or I guess smell would be a better word…that you've found your mate and have given Debra the heave-ho."

"She's your mate." Roger nodded, not really paying attention to his brother, only focusing on the door that seemed far away. "What were you going to do? Have one of us impregnate her, then pawn it off as my kid?"

Roger stared at his brother. Christ, he'd figured that out as well? Then he laughed. Someone had been very busy, it seemed.

"Your she-wolf, did she fill you with these ideas or did you come up with that one all by yourself?" He moved behind his brother in an attempt to get to the door, but it opened suddenly and there stood a police officer. "Ah, I see, all prepared, are you? Not that it matters. If I wanted through you, I'd simply go."

"You're going to jail. And you're not going to do anything but sit down and write out your statement." Roger moved to the chair as his brother's threat took hold. Putting the key into his mouth, he swallowed it and then let his wolf take him.

Leaping at the cop, Roger swiped at his brother only to miss him. But he'd caught the cop across the chest and knew that his brother would stay to help him rather than chase him down. But Roger hadn't counted on the other cops in the hall, nor the big black wolf that stood there growling at him. If the alpha commanded him to stop, Roger knew he'd have no choice. Turning in the other direction, Roger ran down the hall and crashed through the glass front windows just as someone said his name. The pain in his chest had him flinch away, but he knew if he stopped now, he was as good as dead.

Roger moved to his safe house he'd set up two weeks ago. He'd put everything in it he could think of in the event he had to run, and was now glad he'd thought to put in a medical kit. The fact that he'd not healed when he'd shifted from wolf to human scared him. And when he touched the wound, he knew for sure it was silver.

"You need help?" Roger looked at the man standing in front of him, and it took his pain-filled mind several seconds to figure out who it was.

"Dad?" The man, Al Witt, nodded. "What the hell are you doing here? And how the hell did you find me? I didn't even know you lived in this area."

"I don't. Move to the couch and I'll see if I can dig it out." Roger had to be helped. The loss of blood and the silver in his system was making him sick. As soon as he was lying down, his father continued as if nothing had happened.

"I came here about a week after you and your brother did. I was going to approach him about seeing Andi, but I didn't know how. A man has a right to see his only granddaughter." His shirt was ripped open and even that hurt like hell. "You shot anywhere else besides the chest?"

"No. Don't you think that's fucking enough?" He hissed through the pain until he was cleaned up and they could both see the wound. "Angie. Your granddaughter's name? It's Angela. We all call her Angie though."

He had no idea why it mattered to either of them right now. His dad pulled on gloves as he stared at the wound. "You didn't heal. Do you know why? Is it because the bullet is still in there?"

"It's silver. Silver and wolves don't mix." His dad took out a pair of scissors and held them in his hand. "What the fuck do you think you're going to do with those?"

"Cut you open and take it out. I'm guessing that silver or not you'll heal better without it in there gumming up the works. Are you going to be a pussy and cry or take this like a fucking man?"

It took him an hour of digging and he'd only managed to get most of the bullet out. Roger was sweating like a whore in a church, and blood was soaking the towels around him. Finally Roger let the blackness take him. He was at the point now that he didn't really care if he ever woke up.

He wasn't sure how long he'd been out. The room's lighting didn't change, but the furniture did. Once when he woke, he'd been in so much pain that he'd screamed like the pussy his father had called him. His father was taking him to the bedroom and trying his best, Roger was sure, to hit every wall and doorframe on the way. When his head hit the pillow this time, he didn't so much slide into an unconscious state as much as embrace it.

~~~

"The house has central air as well as a whole house vacuum system. The nine bedrooms are all equipped with their own bathrooms as well as an en suite—"

"Could you give me a minute?" Jade cut off the man showing them around the big house. "I just need to clear up a few things with Mr. Witt." The man smiled at her, and she had a feeling he didn't think she had a brain in her head. When he left, she looked at Angie, then at her dad.

"I know, I know, you want me to go find something to do in another room." Angie glared up at her before continuing. "But you owe me for this. I was looking around this place and I like it."

As she stomped away, Jade had to smile. The girl was as smart-mouthed as anyone she'd ever met. But her father, Jade decided, she wanted to murder. He was looking way too sexy in his tight shirt and tighter jeans. She was distracted for a few seconds when his cock started to harden while she watched. Her chin was lifted up, and Quentin smiled at her.

"You keep looking at me like that and we'll never get to find out what each of the bedrooms has in it. It might be something really special." It took her fogged brain a few seconds to catch up. Quentin laughed when she glared harder.

"What am I doing here and not working? I have a job, you know, and helping you find a house is not on my job description. I should know, I wrote it out." She'd been very proud of that, too. "I know what you're going to say…we're mates and all and I should help you. But I'm pretty sure you're very capable of finding your own house."

"And how will I know if you like it or not?" She looked at him, confused. "You do want a house, right? I don't care for living in an apartment really, but if that's what you want, then—" She looked around the house then back at him as he laughed. "You do like this house, am I right?"

"What's not to like? But I still don't know what you want me here for." Then it occurred to her. "You want me to live here with you?"

"Well, of course I do. Why the hell would I buy a house this big if not to give to my wife?" She looked behind her, sure he was talking about someone else. "Jade, I want to marry you. As soon as it can be arranged as a matter of fact."

"You just met me." He nodded and smiled at her. "You can't want to marry me. I mean, you can want to, but that doesn't mean you should. I have all sorts of things going on with me."

"I know you think that most of them are overwhelming, but they really aren't." He took her into his arms and held her. "This is going to be wonderful. I want to spend the rest of my life getting to know you."

"Are you done telling her yet?" They both looked at the doorway where Angie was standing. "Uncle Sloan is here and he wants to talk to you, Dad. He says it's really important."

Quentin took her hand and they walked to the front of the house again. The real-estate agent was talking to a tall man who Jade assumed was Sloan. But she stopped moving. Then he turned to look at her. Every part of her body was tense, and her wolf was clawing at her skin.

"I'm his friend." The man spoke softly, but she heard him. "I'm not here to hurt you, only to talk to you. I swear to you that I'm not—"

"Angie," Jade snapped. "Come away from him. Come to your father now."

"Jade, what is it?" She didn't stop staring at the other man as Quentin questioned her. She was terrified more than she'd ever been, but the man told Angie to go to her dad. She let a little of her wolf go, and he grinned at her.

"Did you know that her boyfriend was a vampire, Quentin? That Kent Ballard hurt her in more ways than you can imagine?" She shivered when she thought of Kent, but Sloan continued talking without moving in her direction. "That's how he was able to get her personal information. He hurt her for it."

"You don't know what you're talking about." But he did and he was right. "I had it on my computer and he hacked into it."

"I won't hurt you, Jade. I swear to you. I've been a friend of Quentin's since he saved my life a good many years ago. His daughter is like my own, and I'd never do anything to harm either of them. And now that you're his mate, you're family, too." His voice was soothing, and she wondered if he was using some kind of compulsion on her. "I won't do that. Once you get to know me, you'll see that."

"I don't want to get to know you. You're a vampire. Vampires only want one thing and that's to drain people. I'll never submit to you." He nodded and took a step toward the agent. That's when she realized that he was in some sort of trance.

"I didn't want him to see us in the event that you shifted. Nor did I think it prudent that he was privy to our conversation." Sloan glanced at Quentin. "You should tell the man you want the house and send him on his way. I don't think that your mate is going to be able to control her wolf for much longer."

His voice never changed in cadence, but she knew that he wasn't happy with her. Tough shit; she didn't like vamps and certainly didn't care for this man. When he laughed, she knew that he was reading her mind. When he touched it, she staggered back slightly.

"I'm very old and have some powers gifted to me by my maker, who is sadly no longer of this earth. I would like to speak to you openly about Ballard if you'd allow me." She shook her head. *"He's hurting another woman, and will continue on until someone stops him. The last woman he met wasn't as lucky as you were. He killed her when she didn't have enough to give him."*

"He would have killed me, too, had I not been a wolf." He nodded and looked at Quentin when he came back into the hallway with them. *"You hurt him or his little girl and I'll stake you."*

"Agreed." Sloan looked at Quentin when he stood beside her. "Your mate and I have come to an understanding. She'll let me advise you on the issue you had me look into, and I'll live a good deal longer, so long as I don't hurt what is hers."

Jade wanted to deny it, but it was basically the truth. She walked to Sloan and put out her hand. It was a handshake that would change their lives if either of them crossed the line. She'd have his scent, and he'd have hers as well. He seemed to know that she didn't give what was hers easily.

"I'm honored by this." She pulled her hand away and watched as he licked his palm. "Your scent is as good as your blood if I need to find you. And I'm sure you'll do the same."

It wasn't a threat, but it could have been, and they were both aware of it. When Quentin took her hand, she looked at Angie, who tugged on her shirt. The little girl looked bored.

"Are you guys going to be friends or what? I love you both, but I'm not going to let you be mean to each other." Sloan picked her up and kissed her cheek. "You should kiss Jade, too. She's really nice and Daddy loves her."

Jade looked at Quentin when he didn't deny loving her. When he kissed her hand, she expected him to say something glib. But all he did was stare into her eyes.

"We will own the house by tomorrow morning. There are some papers you have to sign but other than that, we can start moving in tomorrow. I don't have a great deal of stuff. How about you?" She shook her head, not sure if she was answering him or trying to clear the cobwebs from her brain. This was too surreal.

"I think we should find a place to talk." Sloan sat Angie down as he spoke. "I have some files, too, that I'd like to go over with you, as well as some information on Roger that you might find useful."

"I need to talk to you about that, too. I think he's on the run." Quentin buckled Angie in the car that he'd rented for them for the day. "He's been shot, too. Silver. Thanks for that bit of information."

"You shot your brother with silver?" He told her a cop did. "Whoa, you had your brother shot? What the hell for? Because he is bonking Debra? Are you still in love with her?"

Quentin kissed her nose before explaining to her. "No to all that. I didn't have him shot. He was shot fleeing the scene of the crime. He's stealing my money by skimming the books. The cop who shot him is a were, too, I only just found out. Did you know that you have about fifty percent of your police force as weres? Never mind. Anyway, as for him bonking Debra? Christ, I'm glad it's him and not me. I'm having enough fun just trying to keep up with you." She flushed and heard Sloan laugh and change it to a sudden coughing fit.

"I was just asking." He kissed her again, and she blushed more. There was something about this man that had her all twisted up in one moment and made her a bowl of Jell-o the next.

The trip to the pack house was made mostly with Angie talking about school and that she had to be registered soon.

Jade was thinking about how she'd been in her first grade and smiled. The little girl was going to be a big hit with the teachers. Jade wondered where she was going when she thought of the man who she'd killed.

"She wanted to go to the school that Emerald was teaching at. I guess she doesn't want to do that now." Quentin glanced at her, then back at the road as she continued. "Emerald said that two of the other kids dropped out because of what had happened."

"She wants to go there. I didn't even try to talk her out of it." Jade looked at Quentin as he continued in a low voice. "Any school that she might want to go to will have something that will scare her. But she likes Emerald and she had a very good time that day despite what had gone down. She said that she needs to go there to protect the others."

"She would too." Quentin asked her if she'd see if Emerald had any room in her class for Angie. "I'm pretty sure she'd make room even if she had to put her at her own desk. Angie was a big hit there."

As they pulled into the drive at the house, she saw her other sisters just getting out of a big car. Jade knew that Opal was out of town at a wholesale market, but it looked like everyone else was there, including Diamond and Thad. She'd not seen her sister since she and Thad had returned from their honeymoon.

Dinner was loud and fun. Each of them had welcomed Sloan with open arms as they had welcomed first Thad, then Quentin. Jade was fixing a plate for Angie when Sloan sat down beside her.

"They don't know, do they?" She didn't bother looking at him or even asking him what he meant. "You might have told your family that Kent was a vamp, but not that he abused you nearly every day when you were together, did you? Why?"

She wanted to tell him that it was none of their business, but that wasn't true either. The real truth was she'd thought she was in love with Kent and that he was her mate. But that had been another part of his abuse, giving her that thought then taking it away when he'd found what he needed. And then when he'd started hurting her, she'd been too embarrassed to tell anyone.

"Because he hurt more than my body. He hurt my pride and my heart." She looked at him then. "I'm going to make him pay if it's the last thing I do."

"Good for you. Now let me tell you what I have on the bastard." Sloan, Blair, Quentin, and Jade all retired to the office after dinner. Several hours later, they still had no working plan, but they did have an agreement. Kent Ballard was going to find out he'd fucked with the wrong girl.

Chapter 8

Roger woke to the sound of a vacuum running. He tried pulling a pillow over his head, but the noise just wouldn't go away. Finally he rolled to his back with the intent to get up and tear the person apart, and felt the wound in his chest tear open and pain radiate throughout his body.

He lay there as still as he could until the pain either killed him or receded. Roger opened his eyes when he smelled someone come into the room. It was his father. The low growl spilled from his lips and his father stopped moving.

"I got you a pain pill and something to eat." Moving a little more into the room, his father set the tray he had in his hands on the dresser next to where he lay. "I brought you some in earlier, but you were still out. I got you a cleaning crew here wiping the place down. Sort of dusty."

"I like it that way." The scent of female hit his nose, and Roger felt his cock stretch. She wasn't his but she'd do. But if he was honest with himself, he wasn't sure what he could do once he got her beneath him. "How long have I been here?"

"Three days. I got most of the silver out, but there's a bit more in there. That bullet tore the hell up when it hit your ribs. I might be able to get it out if I had something to hold you down with, but I'm not going to try it again now." His father turned his head to show the huge bruise that was on his face. "You got me pretty good there once and I damn near let the silver take you, but I'm figuring you have a plan and we might be able to profit off it. This about your brother?"

"Why are you here? And how did you find me?" There was no way that Roger was going to discuss money and his brother with this man. First of all, his father and brother hated each other with a hard passion; and secondly, whatever profit that Roger made was going to be his, not a split with the man who sired them both.

"I went to see that man your brother hung out with, Galloway, and they told me he moved up here about three months ago. I figured if he moved here, your brother can't be far behind. Then I went to see that woman." Roger stilled in reaching for the tray of food when he mentioned a woman. "You remember her, Debra Winters. Heard tell he was sniffing around her."

The tray went flying as Roger leapt at his dad. He wasn't sure if his intent was to kill him or not, but he did hold him against the wall for several minutes until his wolf calmed down. The word "mine" kept pounding in his head, but he doubted his father would understand. When he did finally drop him to the floor, Roger sat back down on the bed and took several deep, slow breaths to keep his animal from getting the better of him. Roger wasn't sure if his dad was aware of his change or not.

"You better get control of that thing or he'll get your ass into trouble." Roger nodded, guessing at some point someone had told him. "I got you some more broth. Didn't know that girl was something to you."

After his father left him, Roger staggered to the bathroom to clean up. There was still blood seeping from his wound and he was weak from it. More than likely from the silver that wasn't removed. Turning on the shower, he reached for Debra just to see where she was. He touched her mind while laughing.

"You have some money burning a hole in your pocket?" She growled at him, and he laughed harder. *"What the hell are you shopping for negligees for? You coming here to model them for me?"*

"No, your brother and that other woman, the wolf, are hooked up. Did you know that? They bought a fucking house together." Roger let the soap he had in his hand slip from his fingers when he heard what she said. *"Not to mention there's a warrant out for your arrest. What the fuck were you doing skimming money from him? Did it ever occur to you that you'd fucking ruin everything for us?"*

"Quentin isn't seeing the girl. She's his mate?" His blood ran colder as he thought of the implications of what his brother might be doing now, especially with a mate that was already a wolf and was related to the alpha. He'd never be able to go back and get what he felt was his.

"How the hell should I know? They have a house near the pack place, or whatever it is you called it, and they have enrolled that brat in the school. Fucking bastards are going to ruin everything for us, aren't they?" They already had, but he didn't say anything to Debra as she continued to rant. *"Then there's the whole thing with that green house. That fucker is making so much money now...hell, Roger, I went there to talk to that bitch and there was a line out the door of people paying. And all of them so happy about it that I wanted to fucking puke."*

"Happy? About what?" He finished with his shower and was drying off when she answered him. How the hell had he managed to get that much inventory? Then he remembered that he'd doubled the orders, thinking to have some fun at his brother's expense. Well, that backfired on him, too.

"I need you to come to my place. Bring a van if you have one. I have to get out of here. And there are some things we need to collect, too. Fucking bastard is going to pay for this." He went into the bedroom naked to see the woman who'd apparently been making his bed turn and stare at him. He stroked his cock but didn't touch her. *"Debra, when you get here, I'm going to fuck you hard, baby. I need to bury my cock in you so deep you'll feel me every time you swallow."*

She moaned, and he reached for the girl. There was no reason he couldn't have a little fun before she got there. And Roger was always up for some fun.

"Suck me." She nodded and dropped to her knees in front of him. When his father came into the doorway, he stared at Roger for several seconds before moving away, but not before pulling the door closed. As soon as the woman closed her mouth over his cock, he rocked hard into her. Christ, he needed this more than he'd thought. Fucking her mouth and thinking of how he was going to kill Quentin had him coming hard after only a few minutes. When she cupped his balls, he moaned.

"You want some of this?" She nodded, her eyes glassy with need. "Lean over the bed and I'll fuck you. But you say a word, one word…." Roger pulled her head up to his mouth and licked the pounding pulse. "…one word and I'll tear your throat out and leave you here for the rats."

"Please." Roger tossed her on the bed and he was slamming his cock into her pussy even as she bounced. He'd only meant to fuck her until he came again, but when she wrapped her legs around his hips, he knew that he had to have more. She whimpered when he licked a path from her throat to her nipple. Then he bit down just hard enough to break the skin. Blood filled his mouth, and he sucked harder. Lifting his head, he looked down at her and smiled.

"You're going to get more than you bargained for, I think." She nodded. "It's really too bad that you picked today to clean here. I can't leave you around as a witness."

He was pounding into her when she started to fight him. It was too late for her, and he was pretty sure she knew it. By the time he was throwing back his head coming deep inside of her, she was already as close to death as it came. Roger tore out her throat as the last of his cum shot from him, and he licked the blood up almost as fast as it poured from her throat. Sated and feeling better than he had in a while, Roger went back to the shower to clean up again. He was dressing when someone knocked on the door.

His dad opened the door when he bid him entrance. He looked at the bed, then at him. There was something there in his eyes, but Roger wasn't sure what it was. At first he'd thought it was horror, but then he thought he saw a gleam in his eyes. Could it be that his dad was a sadist, too?

"Good thing I got that whore with a stolen credit card or you'd be cleaning this mess up." Roger nodded, not sure what to say at this point. "Come on. Her car is still here and we can use it until something better comes along. Oh, and I already took her money. No cards, but that might be pushing it a bit."

They were in the car driving toward the mall where Debra was when he thought of his brother. There was going to be hell to pay on his end, and Roger could not wait to make him pay up.

"Quentin has taken on a mate. A very wealthy and very powerful mate. The alpha's family as a matter of fact." His dad nodded. "I might be able to dodge them for a little while, but Quentin has my scent all over his business and they'll be able to track me. I have to lay low for a while."

"I got just the place. I've been holed up there for a few weeks. There's power and water, but nothing fancy. Got me a bed, too, but we can work out getting something more. The entire building is empty of people but filled to the top with shit that nobody's been using for a while." Roger nodded. "And so you know, that girl you just killed, she's with some service. They'll be looking for her sooner or later. The house in your name?"

"No." Roger laughed. "I put it in Debra's. Boy, she's going to be pissed when they come knocking on her door." He was still laughing when they got to the abandoned apartment complex. His dad told him he'd show him around then go out for some food.

"Most of the lower windows are knocked out, but I've got me a nice place on the upper floor. Kitchen and fridge. Not sure why the power is still running here, but there you have it." As they entered, his dad continued telling him about what else he'd discovered. "It was slated to be torn down about six years ago, but for some reason it's still here. Budgets, I guess."

The elevator even worked, and they rode it up in relative ease. When it came to a smooth stop at the upper floor, Roger got out. The place was…nice, he guessed. His dad had done a good job cleaning the place up.

"I had to sneak in a few things that I took. Like the sweeper. It was something I needed, so I took it. Same with the plates and stuff. Microwave was a little harder to come by, but I was able to get it fairly easy." He smiled at him as if he'd just won the lottery. "People hanging out their laundry gave me my linens and stuff."

The apartment that he was led to wasn't locked, and his dad explained that the keys had been taken. "I've got this one here and you can have the one across from me. I cleaned it up, but it doesn't have the right things yet. We'll work on getting you that as we go. Also, there isn't a phone here. I don't have much use for one anyway, but I pick me up one here and there if I need it."

Roger went to the couch as soon as his dad uncovered it. It was ugly in a cheap apartment sort of way, but it wasn't too bad. He laid his head back and closed his eyes. This was something he could get used to, he supposed. When he heard his dad talking, he looked at him and realized he was calling someone. He was telling them about the car that had been abandoned with the key in it and told them to have at it. Nice way to get rid of the evidence, Roger thought. He wondered if he'd ever have any energy again. Closing his eyes, Roger let sleep take him.

~~~

"When?" Quentin sat down at his desk and wondered how the hell this had happened. His father was out of prison. "You said he'd been released. When and how the hell does something like this happen without someone telling me?"

"He was released a month ago. And we're still trying to figure out how it happened. There was a mix-up with his name and—"

"No fucking shit there was a mix-up. He was supposed to serve two life sentences then serve twenty for grand theft and all the things he did to me. What the fuck are you doing down there? Do you have shit for brains?" Jade put out her hand and he slammed the phone into it. This was beyond stupid. And now who knew where his father was and what the fuck he was doing? He listened to Jade speak to the man from the prison.

"Yes, I understand, but he's under a little stress right now. I said I understand, but that in no way makes what happened less incredibly stupid." She sat down and picked up a pen. "Give me your name. Because when we take the state of Texas to court when your mistake kills someone else, then we'll have a list of the idiots that let him go. So, you refuse to give me that information. No problem. I'll send my sister down there to speak to you. You'll wish to Christ you had done it then. In fact you'll be beg...what's that? Oh yes, that would be very helpful. I'll give you an email address to send it to."

He watched her recite her email address to him and hang up. "What did you just get from him? I'm assuming the threat of your sister coming down there scared him just a little."

"Yes, he knows Sapphire apparently. She called him earlier today when I let her know what was going on. I think he's afraid of her. I would be too, if I had to tangle with her as a human." She stood up and went to his side of the desk and sat on his lap. "He's going to send me the names of all the people who worked there and their department. I'm not sure that's legal or anything, but we'll have it. I'm thinking we can look it over and pick out a couple of names and see what they might know. Someone let your dad out."

"Daddy?" They both looked at the doorway when Angie stepped in. When Jade tried to stand up, he held her on his lap. She was much too comfortable where she was anyway and stayed put for him.

"Yes, love. What can I do for you on this fine morning?" She skipped across the room toward them and crawled up into Jade's lap. Quentin could get used to this and decided he would.

"I need to go school shopping. I don't have any pants to wear to my new school, and Emerald gave me a list of supplies I would have to have. She said I could catch up with the other kids when I get them." Angie snuggled into Jade's throat as she continued. "I don't suppose you can take me, can you, Jade? Daddy doesn't like shopping for little girl stuff. He told me it's unmanly."

Both of them laughed. "What I said was it's unmanly to have to go into those stores with all those screaming little preteens that have no idea what they're wearing is nothing but cheap merchandise with a brand name on it." Jade looked at him with a frown, as did his daughter. "What? It's the truth."

"Maybe, but don't be a father." Jade looked at Angie. "We'll go tomorrow morning if you want. I think I can convince my sisters to go, too. Not all of them but some. We can get a gift for Sapphire, too. She's going to tell us they're going to have a baby soon and I want to be ready."

Quentin had a thought of Jade large with their child. He wondered if he could have a child with her and decided the next time he had some time, he was going to read that book that Thad had told him about. Other than skimming over it, he'd not had a great deal of time to read much. When someone knocked on the door, he lifted both the women off his life up and sat them on the chair. Sloan stood there with a large file, a laptop, and several bags of food.

"I came bearing gifts." Quentin took the food and then invited him in. He'd nearly forgotten about that until Sloan cleared his throat.

Jade and Angie came into the room a few seconds later. Angie went straight to her favorite uncle. Jade was still a little standoffish, but she was coming around. Quentin told Sloan what she'd done about the prison. He was laughing even before he got to the part where the email was being sent.

"Good job. I had to go and steal what little I have." They sat down to eat the Chinese food while Sloan explained what he had. "Your father was released thirty-seven days ago and went to see Thad. I'm not sure what he wanted with him, but

I think it was to find out where you were. He eventually made his way to here. And as of yesterday, he's off the grid."

"Off how?" Jade was eating an egg roll dripping in sweet and sour sauce, and Quentin wanted to lick the droplets off her. When she growled at him, he felt his cock fill. When she touched his mind, he nearly took her to the floor. *"Behave."*

"I can't. Christ, you look good enough to eat. And I want to. Starting with your pretty pussy and working my way up your body to your breasts. I love how your nipples harden when I touch them." He looked at Sloan when he cleared his throat. Fuck, he'd forgotten they had company. "Sorry. I get wrapped up in her."

"Understandable. She's very beautiful and smart." Sloan looked at her, then back at him. "I've taken the liberty of having your new home warded. I know a few...*people* let's call them, and they have done this to keep you guys safe for me. The only way a person can enter your home is if you both allow it. Angie will need to be cautioned about this, too, as she won't be able to have her friends over until you okay them."

Quentin thanked him. "We're moving in tomorrow. Most of the furniture has been delivered from Texas, and Jade and I have to decide what we're keeping. Then we'll need to fill the rest of the house out. There's a suite in the basement that has your name on it if you want it."

"I saw it. It's a lair." Quentin nodded at him. Jade had told him that several vampires had stayed there, but none were killed. Nor did she believe anyone had been killed down there by them. She'd only smelled small amounts of blood.

"There's something else you should be made aware of. There was a murder, and I believe your brother was involved in it. I don't have your father's scent, but there was a male there as well. As well as Debra's scent." Quentin looked at his daughter and soon-to-be wife and wondered if he could keep them safe. "Quentin, we'll get him. And your father. They won't be able to hide from me."

"I know you will. Blair said the same thing to me yesterday when I told him about my brother. He seemed to think he'd be dead by now. Silver kills their kind." Quentin started cleaning up the mess as he continued. "I hate to wish this, but I wish Roger would just simply go away. I've never forgiven him for the part he played in Isabel's death."

"He'll pay. I assure you he will." Quentin nodded at his friend. He was afraid. Not for himself but his family. Jade had enough stress going on with this Kent person. And now this. He watched her kiss Angie good-bye as she started out the door to work. He didn't want her to leave.

"I have people watching her," Sloan said after she'd kissed him and left. "They'll keep an eye on her all day while I rest. She'll be safe."

Quentin laughed. "She's going to be pissed when she finds out. And she will, mark my words. She can be a tad on the pissy side when she thinks someone is taking care of her. Trust me. I know."

"They'll be careful not to let her know it's going on." Sloan nodded. "You'd be surprised at the kind of people I know."

Quentin would bet, but it made him no less happy to know that when Jade figured it out, he was going to watch every second of her kicking the big vampire's ass. And Quentin had no doubt that she would, too. And he was going to laugh his ass off.

Chapter 9

Kent opened his eyes knowing that someone had come into his lair. Not that he was worried they'd hurt him. Seldom did anyone come to him with anything more than a need that they thought he could provide them answers for. Usually it was only a request to become a vampire, but lately….

"Who dares come to my chamber at this time of day?" No one said anything, but he could hear them breathing. Sniffing the air, he could smell a great deal about this person. "A female human who is mated to a wolf? Can't be good for him if you're stepping out on him already. What do you want?"

"I want you to kill someone for me. And I'm willing to do just about anything to make that happen." She moved out of the shadows and he could see her now. "Even letting you have my body."

"It wouldn't be just your body I'd want, and I'm pretty sure you know that." She moved closer and he could see her. "And though it is a very nice one, I'm still not going to agree to anything without details."

Kent rose from his bed, levitated actually, and floated toward her as he lowered himself to the floor. When she took a step back, he smiled. Nothing made the blood better tasting to him than fear. And even though she was putting up a great front, she was terrified out of her mind.

"It's not terribly smart of you to come to a vampire's lair when he first arises. I have little control over my hunger right now." Which was a lie, but he wanted her more fearful of him. "Say what you want after I've had my fill of you."

Leaning to her throat, he licked her flesh. She was ripe for the plucking, he thought, and he wanted very much to fuck this bitch. Pulling her body to his, he felt her relax against him, but he wasn't fooled. A dagger or a bit of wood could be hidden anywhere on her body. Jerking her head back, he looked into her eyes and captured her.

"Why are you here?" She repeated what she'd said before. "And you found me how? I'm not exactly in the phone book."

"I found you through a friend of a friend. Your name was mentioned in connection with someone I know, the woman I want you to kill as a matter of fact." Kent let his fangs show, and she swallowed hard. Fear and arousal now spiked her blood. "Are you going to bite me? I think I'd like whatever you want from me as much as you want it."

Kent smiled and leaned down to sniff her. No poisons, though it wouldn't harm him, but he did smell the wolf. Licking the pounding pulse, he bit down on her throat and drank deeply from her. His cock swelled with the fresh blood.

She grabbed onto his shoulders as her climax took her. He'd not given her that thought, but she'd come all the same. Moving her back toward his bed, he drank more from her until he had all his strength back. Lifting his head after sealing the wound, he looked at her again.

"Strip off all your clothes and stand before me." He sat on the bed to watch her. "Faster. I want to feel your pussy around my cock, and I want it now."

She nearly tore her clothes off in her haste. When she stood before him naked, he pulled her closer to him and took her nipple into his mouth and bit her again. Blood filled his mouth, and she curled her fingers into his hair and held him to her. Christ, she was as willing as he'd ever had. Pushing her away, he told her to drop to her knees.

"Suck my cock while I think about what you want." She eagerly did as he said and had his cock in her mouth almost as soon as she touched him. He surged up until she would either swallow him or choke. She swallowed. "I think I'm going to keep you for a while. You might prove to be quite entertaining."

The moan that spilled from her throat had him fucking her harder. She was good, and he found he wanted to know if her pussy was just as hot as her mouth. When he jerked her up from his throbbing cock she reached for him again, and he tossed her to the bed.

"Get down on your knees and present me with your ass. I want to fuck you." She scrambled to the middle of the bed and assumed the position he wanted. Getting on the bed behind her, he could smell how hot she was. Next time, he promised himself, he was going to eat her pussy first. As he slammed into her, she moaned again and he leaned over her to take her like the animal she was.

Fucking someone like this was seldom for the person beneath him. Kent took her hard and when she started to slide her fingers into her pussy, he let her. If she came, her blood would be all the sweeter for it. As soon as his balls began to fill, ready for him to come, he nuzzled into her throat again and bit her. When she screamed and tightened around him, Kent let his own climax roar out of him. But he wanted more.

As soon as he pulled free of her, he rolled her to her back and moved down to her pussy. He could smell his own cum along with hers and he wanted to taste it. Dropping to her pussy, he pressed his finger into her ass at the same time he bit down on her clit. She screamed again and flooded his mouth with her cream and blood. Kent drank quickly, not wanting to miss a drop of either. He brought her to three more quick climaxes while he had his fill. Then he sat up and lifted her onto his cock. Taking her to the bed again, he came deep inside of her, biting her once again at her throat. Christ, he'd never had a human fulfill him so well before. When he rolled off her and sat on the edge of the bed, she didn't move. Leaving her where she lay, he went to the shower to clean up.

"You said you wanted to keep me around. If that's what I can expect, I'm all for it." Her voice floated over the shower doors and he had to smile. He would be deciding if that's what she got or not, and the sooner she learned that the better. Kent threw back the curtain and told her to get in.

"Wash me. I want you to wash every part of my body clean of your stench." She licked her lips and reached for the sponge. "And when you're finished with me, I want you to suck my cock until I come down your throat."

Taking the soap off the shelf, she filled the sponge with it. When she started to rub it over his chest and shoulders, Kent closed his eyes and let her. As soon as she had him turn around, Kent was thinking of ways he could take her in here when she pressed the sponge between his ass cheeks and then over his balls. His cock was aching again.

Turning around, she dropped to her knees and began washing his thighs, then his hips. Fluid leaked from the tip of his cock, and she thumbed it off and put it into her mouth. He had to lean back against the wall as she scrubbed him clean. When he commanded her to service him, she took his cock into her mouth and sucked hard at his crown. Kent watched her as she bobbed up and down over him until he nearly begged her to finish him.

Curling his fingers into her hair, he held her to him as he fucked her mouth. Cupping his balls with her warm, wet fingers, he cried out when she gave them a sharp twist. His climax nearly took him off his feet when it hit him, and he fucked her mouth until he was drained. Pulling her off him, he lay back against the wall and looked at her.

"Who do you want dead? And so you know, the wolf you were sleeping with is not to touch you again. If I have to, I'll kill him to be sure he doesn't." She seemed to consider this and nodded. "You're okay with me killing him so that I can have you?"

"Yes. He fucked me over, and the police are looking for me in question of the woman I'm pretty sure he raped and killed. The fucking bastard can rot in hell for all I care now for all the problems he's caused me." She looked at his cock that, despite coming four times, was still hard and ready. "Besides, I'm thinking you're just what I need sexually. I've never ever come like that with him before."

Kent picked her up by her throat and smiled when she struggled. "And you never will again if you compare me to that bastard again. Understand?"

When she nodded, he dropped her to the floor and turned off the water. Reaching for the towel that lay on the back of the toilet, he dried off and went to the bedroom. Kent was pulling on a shirt when she came out with the same towel wrapped around her body. The bruise at her neck was just forming.

He told her to tell him just what she wanted. "Her name is Jade Erickson, and she's mated to the man that I wanted for my own. I was with his brother, Roger, but as I've said...are you all right?"

"Jade Erickson who has a sister named Sapphire and a few others?" The woman nodded at him. "Mother fuck, you're kidding me. You want me to hunt down the one woman in the world that got away? Gladly."

Kent stood up and pulled his clean shirt off and tossed it to the bed. He wanted to hurt Jade right now, but the woman in front of him would have to do. When she took a step back, he jerked the towel off her and pulled her to him. This time she would not find him as enjoyable as she had before. Biting into her throat, he lifted her over his cock and took her to the wall. When she moaned, he decided that he might be wrong about her. Maybe this woman would enjoy whatever he did to her. Christ, he hoped so, because he had a powerful need to fuck something hard and painfully.

~~~

"I don't know. What do you think?" Jade looked at the outfit that Angie wanted, then at her sister Ruby. She shook her head and smiled. "I think it's a little too...a little too...."

Words failed her, and she looked around the store for some sort of help. The cashiers were running around like they were outfitting a group for war, and the mothers of the other little girls looked like they were on some sort of mission and damn you if you got in the way. Sapphire cleared her throat and leaned into Angie. The little girl's haunted look disappeared, and she smiled for the first time since entering the place. Jade tossed the dress that was, as far as she was concerned, hideous and followed Sapphire and Angie out.

"What do you suppose she said to her?" Jade shrugged at Ruby's question. "Do you think we'll have to come back here? Because I gotta tell you, this place is scarier than my first night in the emergency room."

Jade agreed with her. They caught up with the other two a few minutes later standing in line at the ice cream shop. Both of them were looking at the menu like it was going to give them the answers to all of life's questions. When Angie took her hand, Jade felt as if the sun shone down on her and she could tackle most anything.

"I think Aunt Sapphire is right," Angie told her when they sat down with their treats. "That place is for cows. I'm not part of a.... What did you say?"

"Herd, sweetie, you're not part of a herd but your own person. I think we could go down to that new shop on Seventh Street and find you much better dresses and you could have your own style. Those girls in that shop are cattle and you're going to run the lot of them." Jade didn't know if that was good advice or not but didn't comment. A few minutes later both Diamond and Emerald joined them.

"I'm supposed to tell you that you're not to eat dinner. I guess we're all getting together at your house later." Jade looked around when Emerald pointed to her. "You did get a call from Quentin, right? He said he was going to call you."

"I don't have a phone. And right now it's on my list way at the bottom. I have to get some clothes for work, and there's this car I want that Bubby is selling. It's ugly as sin, but it runs great." She looked at her sisters, who were staring at her as if she had two heads. "What?"

"Okay, you do know that the man who has just bought you a house has more money than both Thad and Blair does, right?" Jade shrugged at Sapphire. "Not to mention he's told you repeatedly that he wants to buy you a car and a phone and whatever else you want."

"I can take care of myself." Sapphire snorted, and Emerald laughed. "I don't know what you think is so funny.

You didn't want Blair buying you whatever he wanted either. I'm not used to having anyone want to buy me stuff, okay?"

"Come on, we're getting you a cell phone right now." Sapphire pulled out her phone and handed it to her. "Call Quentin and have him tell you what company he has a plan on. We'll hit them on the way out."

The phone rang in her hand before she could tell her sister no. She nearly dropped it twice trying to give it back to her sister when she kept saying for her to answer it. Jade glared at Sapphire when she finally figured out how to get the stupid thing to work.

"Just the woman I wanted to talk to." Quentin laughed as he continued. "I was wondering what time you're planning to leave the mall, and also if you'd meet me at the house when you're done."

"Right now we're sitting in the food court having an ice cream and a drink. We just got started on the list but we're going to the Munchkin on Seventh. A friend of Sapphire's owns it and they specialize in kids clothes. Is that okay?" He assured her it was. "Then we have to go to Wal-Mart to get the list of supplies she needs. Do you need for me to bring Angie back to you now?"

"No. She needs this and the two of you need to get used to doing things together. Besides, I think she's having fun with you. She already loves you. I was wondering because I wanted to track you down. I'm having something delivered to you." Confused, she asked him if he wanted her to come and get it. "No, love, there's a man going to bring you a bag. It's a cell phone as well as a few other things I would like for you to have."

"What sort of things?" He laughed and she flushed. "I'm sure whatever it is I can get it later. I don't want you to be bothered with having someone bring it to me here."

"He should be about to you if you're in the food court. His name is Donny and he will show you identification if you ask for it." She saw a man coming toward her with a large bag. "And when I send you things like I'm sure you thought I was sending you, I'd not do it in a busy mall but in the privacy of our bedroom. By the way, our bed came today. We'll break it in later."

Donny was smiling at her and handed her the bag. Before she could ask him, he pulled out his driver's license and showed it to her, as well as his badge that said he worked for Witt Corporations. He told her he was there to answer any questions she might have.

She pulled out the little box and opened it to find a fully charged phone and a note attached to it. It said that all the numbers she needed for now were programmed in. She looked at Quentin's smiling face when it started ringing.

"I guess it works. The other things in the bag are to keep you safe. I know you're all bad assed and can probably protect me better than I can you, but I wanted you to see the pictures of the people I want you to keep an eye out for." She thumbed through the pictures and handed them to her sister as he told her what else was with the bag. Jade pulled out the last box and stared at it for several seconds before she realized Quentin was speaking to her.

"What did you do?" He laughed. "I'm serious. If this is what I think it is, you can just take it back. I have a car that I'm buying. It's not like this one, but it's something I can afford."

"You can afford this one, too. Plus, if you and Angie go out, I want to be sure you'll be okay if someone tries to hurt you. I don't want a thing to happen to either of the women in my life." She started to protest again, but he cut her off. "I want you to have this because I've fallen in love with you and want to give you the world. The car is nothing compared to what I'd like to give you. Please let me do this for you."

Jade wasn't sure what to say. She looked up at Donny, who was looking around like he expected someone to attack. Either that or he was going to go with them to that store again. Shuddering, she asked Quentin.

"He's going to go with you at a safe distance. I think if you send him into the store I think you're talking about, he might quit." He laughed with her this time. "My father and brother are out there, and I don't want to take the chance that they might try to hurt what is mine."

"Am I yours, Quentin?" She flushed when she realized what she'd said. "I'm sorry. That was a stupid question. I wasn't fishing, I swear it. You just said you thought you were falling in love with me and I have to be stupid and—" She stopped talking when he said her name.

"I'm wrong. I'm not falling in love with you. I'm head-over-heels in love with you. And I know you weren't fishing. That's what makes you asking so wonderful."

Tears filled her eyes as she tried to control her emotions. She was in love with him, too, but was too overwhelmed with everything to say anything to him now. When she nodded, knowing he couldn't see her, she felt his laughter. Then he spoke to her through their link.

"I can feel you. It's as if you're touching me with your love and it's all around me. I've never felt anything so...so overwhelming before. Is this really how you feel about me, love?"

"Yes," she told him as she ended the call. *"I've never loved anyone before. Never, and to be honest with you it terrifies me a great deal. It's almost too hard to believe."* He sent her his love, and it wrapped around her like a warm blanket and filled her up. *"Oh Quentin, I do love you."*

"*And I love you.*" He laughed again. "*I'm beginning to see why you'd not gotten a cell phone before this. Is this the way you speak to everyone? It's amazing.*"

"*Not everyone, just family and now you. But as you know, I couldn't afford it before now.*" She stood when the others did to move out. "*Will Donny be driving Angie and me around? I don't want to make him quit if we go to another store.*"

"*He'll be fine. Donny has been my body guard for a very long time. Since before my father did —* " She could feel his anger and wondered about it. "*We have to talk about my father and why he's no longer a part of my life. Tonight, all right? We, you and I, will sit down and talk about a lot of things.*"

She told him it would be fine. Moving out the doors to the parking lot, she saw the car immediately. It was a car only in the sense that it had doors and four wheels. The rest was…well, she wasn't sure. It was the biggest SUV that she'd ever seen, and it was hot cherry red.

"Oh yeah, no one will notice you coming." Sapphire laughed as she crawled into the back seat with her and Angie. "It's much nicer than the one that Blair and I have. I might have to have him outdo you."

"Please don't. This is…it's too much." Sapphire took her hand as her other sisters got in as well. "I don't want all this."

"But you need it and you most assuredly deserve it. Enjoy it, love. Men like our mates aren't the norm. We are very, very lucky." Jade nodded at her. "Now, let's go and spend some money."

Holy Christ, Jade felt as if she was in big trouble here.

Chapter 10

Quentin was looking over the spread sheet for the newest project he was thinking of getting involved in when his phone rang. He barely glanced at the caller ID and answered it. There were so many people calling him over the past three days that he was getting irritated. He had to hire someone to answer his phone.

"Mr. Witt, Quentin Witt?" The voice sounded nervous. He picked up a pen to write down anything he might say. It was important, he knew, that if someone was going to threaten you to have as much detail for the police as possible.

"This is him. Who is this and what do you want?" The man didn't say anything for several seconds, and Quentin nearly hung up.

"This is Doctor James at County General. Do you by chance know a Miss Debra Winters?" Quentin felt his body drain, and he went lax against his seat. His first thoughts were that Roger had killed her, too.

"I do. What's happened to her? I'm not her family, but I will—"

"No. I realize that." Doctor James cut him off. "She's told us that and…she wants to see you. I mean really wants to see you. She's been here since last night and, frankly, I'm not sure how she's survived this long. But she is screaming for you. She said she needs to see you right now." The doctor took a deep breath. "I'm sorry to tell you this over the phone, but if you could see your way here as soon as possible, it might ease her way. She's...she's not well."

Quentin grabbed his coat from the back of his chair and asked the man to repeat where he was going. "I don't know this area well, so if you could give me the address, I could get there much quicker."

"Yes, she said you'd just moved here from Texas." The doctor told him how to get there as well as the address. "Sir, do you know if she has a next of kin we can notify as well? You see she's only said your name and that she needed to talk to you. She's afraid that you'll...she said that you might not come but that I was to convince you to be here."

"I'll be there. Tell her I'm on my way." He was moving out the door to the elevator when he realized that his brother might be there and asked the doctor if she had anyone there now.

"No, she was found in the parking lot yesterday afternoon and brought into the emergency room. One of the doctors here was able to find out her name by recognizing her from the paper." Quentin reached for Blair to see how to contact Diamond or Ruby to see if this might be a trap. "I'm going in to assure her now that you're coming."

Quentin ended the call just as Blair reached him back. *"I'm on my way out the door. Good job on using your new skills. I was — "*

"I'm so sorry, but I need to contact one of the others at the hospital. I just got a call from a Doctor James and he said that Debra was there and in bad shape. How do I...? I don't know...do this with them?"

"You can't," Blair told him, and Quentin pulled out his phone to figure out how to call them. *"But I can. You head on over to the hospital and I'll get in touch with Diamond. She is in charge over there and can get more information than anyone I know."*

Five minutes later, Blair confirmed that Debra was there and was indeed in bad shape. *"She's lost a great deal of blood, but the doctors don't know how. They think she's bitten herself."*

"But you don't think so." Blair said he didn't. *"Do you think that my brother bit her so badly that she's bleeding to death? Doesn't someone have to seal those kinds of bites?"*

"They do, but I don't know that it was him. Diamond is checking on her now. But you should hurry. There really isn't a great deal of time left."

Quentin was shown to a room that was not a normal hospital room. The walls were all windows and there was a guard outside the room that didn't look like anyone he'd fuck with. When the nurse showed him to the room, the guard stepped back but not far enough where he could no longer reach him. Quentin stepped into her room to find Diamond there already. Debra lay quietly on the bed.

"She's resting for now, but she'll wake soon. She's having nightmares, she said." Diamond moved closer to him. "Debra's been bitten by a vampire, and most if not all the bites have not been sealed. She's lost too much blood and refuses a transfusion. I'm sorry, Quentin, she's going to die if she doesn't get help."

"Quentin? Is that you?" He moved closer to the bed and turned back to Diamond when she nodded. Christ, the woman in the bed looked nothing at all like the Debra he knew.

Her skin was pasty white and brittle looking. Her lips, which had once been full and lush, looked dried and cracked, pale as her face. The colors of her eyes were faded to almost clear and were sunken so deep into her head that she looked dead already.

"I'm here." He almost took her hand, but Diamond told him not to. "Did Roger do this to you? I'll kill him if he did."

Her laugh was maniacal. Quentin felt it like nails down a chalk board. There was something very off about this, and he was afraid for Jade and his daughter.

"I contacted him. You told me his name once, I think, or maybe you told Roger. Things are fuzzy now." She closed her eyes for a second. "He's coming for you...not you but that woman you're fucking. He wants her dead because he didn't kill her before and he likes to hurt people."

"Who?" But he had a feeling he already knew who. And the why. He started to ask her how she'd met him when she threw back the sheets. "Mother fuck, Debra, did Ballard do this to you?"

Bites. All over her body that he could see. When she pulled her gown up, they were there on her belly and breasts. Her arms looked like she'd taken a razor to them, just like her legs. Even her feet were bitten, her toenails black from them. Some of them bled still, while others seeped out something that didn't look like anything but pus. He started to take a step back, but she grabbed him. Her grip was very strong for as weak as she appeared.

"He's going to kill her, then you. Kent will kill Angie, too. Not that I liked the brat, but I'd never want him to do to her what he's done to me. And he will." She closed her eyes and he could see she was straining to stay with him. "He's going to kill you all, but you have to kill him first."

"I will." She dropped her hand and laid there. Before he could ask her if she needed anything, she bowed up off the bed and screamed. Quentin started to reach for her but

Diamond threw him back just in time. Debra screamed once more. Then she exploded.

Quentin was still sitting in the hallway waiting for someone to tell him he could leave when someone touched his arm. He looked up to find Blair there and Jade running down the hall toward him. Quentin stood up and went to her, grabbing her up in his arms and holding her.

"They said you weren't hurt, but I didn't believe them." Quentin kissed her mouth, neck, and cheeks. "I have to see you."

When she pulled back from him, he still held her hand. After what seemed an eternity, she was satisfied and let him hug her again. They were still holding each other when Sloan appeared beside them.

"It was Ballard. He found that she was talking to someone, I would imagine, and he killed her. I would say that she was in a great deal of pain when he did it, too." Sloan looked back toward the room and then back at him. "I have his scent now as well as his blood from the girl. She'd been…he'd turned her most of the way and by the next moon, she would have been a vampire like him."

"Evil you mean?" Sloan nodded at Jade. "What can we do to stop him? We have to do something before he hurts someone else. No one should suffer like that poor woman did."

Sloan looked like he wanted to tell her no, but he looked at her family then back at her. Quentin wouldn't want to face any of them if he had to, not as a foe. Sloan seemed to understand that.

"I would like to suggest some things first. Some you might be all right with, others…well, they are things that could help you all." He nodded toward a room, and Quentin and she followed him. As soon as the door shut behind them, he sat on the bed and started talking.

"I would like to suggest that you convert Quentin. It will help him in the long run. When you're both wolves, there are things you can do as a mated couple that you cannot as a human and wolf." Quentin nodded before Jade could say anything. "Secondly, you should both think about having the little girl have a body guard. Even at the school. She's the one that I would take to control you, and she's ripe for the picking."

"Ripe for the picking? I'm not sure I know what that means." Quentin looked at Jade when Sloan didn't answer him. "Do you know?"

"He means she's too trusting. She'd go with someone without thought to whether or not they'd hurt her." She looked at him as she continued. "Kent or even your family could tell her she was doing something you wanted her to, and she'd willingly go with them."

He wanted to deny it but really wasn't sure. She was very trusting and was friendly, too. And someone evil, like this Ballard person, would exploit her just to get what he wanted. Quentin looked at Sloan.

"What else? You want something else, what is it?" He stood up and walked toward them. Quentin was suddenly very afraid.

"I would very much like to have your permission to bite you both, and Angie." Jade said no almost immediately, but he watched him. "I can find you, all of you, if he takes you. I will also be able to talk to you through a link that will let me know if you're hurt or afraid. I will find you if he takes you, any of you."

"And how much will you need?" Jade moved away from him and he could feel her anger. He could understand her to a point, but he didn't want anything to happen to any of them. But Sloan's way would insure that they had a better chance of getting out alive.

"A sip." Jade left the room, and Sloan sat down. "I won't hurt her. I know that she doesn't believe that, and, frankly, I can understand that, but I won't ever harm her. You know that." He did, too.

"I'll talk to her. In the meantime, take mine and we'll—"

Sloan told him he couldn't do that unless his mate approved. "She's going to be mad at me anyway. If I take your blood, even freely given, she will hate us both. And as your mate she can't hurt you, but she can make your life a living hell if you cross her." Quentin thought that Sloan might be right. "I am."

"She'll come around. I'll talk to her." Sloan nodded. "I will ask her about Angie, too. I don't want her to ever think that Angie is anything but our daughter from now on."

"Good idea. Have you told her about Isabel yet? It might help her." Quentin shook his head, and Sloan nodded. "It's up to you, but the reason I ask is that if she knew what your father's part in her death was about, she'd be more inclined to take care with the child. And this time I'm going to find him and he will no longer be a threat."

Sloan disappeared after that. Quentin paced the room for several minutes before he moved out into the hall with the others. He was handed his clothes in a large plastic bag and told that he could keep the scrubs they'd given him. Thanking the nurse, he went to find his family because regardless of blood, they were his family.

On the way back to his house, he asked them all to stay for a while. He had something to tell them. All of them agreed, and Annabelle said she'd bring some steaks, too.

119

Quentin was about to tell them of his first wife, and he didn't want to have to tell this story ever again if possible.

"Isabel Cole was Angie's mother." Angie sat down in Jade's lap as they sat around the living room in the big house that Blair told him was the pack house. "She and I didn't love each other, but we married because Angie was on the way."

He'd told Angie that he and her mother had loved her very much, but the two of them just were not in love with each other. They got along and may have eventually fallen in love, but soon after their daughter was born, she was murdered.

"My father did it. And though I was never able to prove it, I think that Roger had something to do with it as well. He, Roger, was brought in for questioning, but nothing ever became of it." Quentin started pacing. "We'd been home from the hospital for about two weeks when my father came by to see the baby. I had kicked him out of my life when I'd turned eighteen for lots of reasons, but mostly because I no longer trusted him. It wasn't just money, because at the time I had very little. It was because he was a thief as well as a man who lived on the wrong side of life, and was just about to take the plunge into being nothing I wanted to have anything to do with. Especially now that I had a family."

"But he didn't back off, did he?" Quentin shook his head at Blair's question. "How did she die?"

"Strangulation. He tied her up to the beams in our house and held her on a chair. He said it was an accident, that he'd only wanted to teach me a lesson. But she'd slipped off while he was out making some other deal and died. She was there for five days before we found her, because Dad had skipped out when he realized what he'd done." Quentin stopped pacing and looked around the room for a second before continuing. "He told us this in the courtroom. Dad had been his own attorney and couldn't fathom why we, anyone for that matter, would find any of this his fault. It had been a surprise to us then, and Angie got to hear her grandfather tell us that he'd killed her but it wasn't his fault."

"Bastard." A notion that Quentin agreed with wholeheartedly and told Diamond that when she spoke. "And now he's out of prison. Do we have any idea why?"

"I do." They all looked at Jade. "I've been looking into it. It seems it really was a mistake and the prison system is doing everything they can to make it right. Your father's social ends in seven three nine four. The numbers of the man they were supposed to release were seven nine three four. They transposed two of the numbers and didn't catch it. When I called them back, I found out that prior to his untimely release, there have been five total that have been released under the same mistake, each of them done by the same person."

"Well I hope to Christ they fired this person." Jade shook her head at Blair. "Don't tell me they gave them retirement and let them go without even a smack on the wrist? That would really piss me off."

"Everything pisses you off, love." Sapphire kissed her husband on the cheek as she continued. "Hush now and let her finish. Can't you see she had the whole story?"

"No, he's been fired until an investigation can be performed and does not get paid. It's the deal that Quentin and his lawyers worked out. If no one is found to be guilty of purposely letting these prisoners out, then he and the other families that have been victimized, as well as the prisoners that weren't released, won't sue."

Blair looked at him and smiled. "I'm impressed. Way to make things work for you. This way they'll find him quicker by working harder and you don't have to do all the leg work all by yourself. I think I'm going to like having you as a brother in arms."

"Speaking of which." Quentin walked toward Jade and dropped to his knees in front of her. "I've wanted to do this for several days now, but I've been sort of looking for the right ring. It's been my mission to give you something that symbolizes what I feel for you."

Angie walked up behind him and put her hand on his shoulder. He'd asked her if this was okay with her and she had a lot of questions, most of which centered on having a mom and maybe a sister or two. "No boys," she'd told him. "They stink."

"I want you to be my wife, and Angie would very much like for you to be her mom. She's not had one really and is excited to see if you'll do okay." He winked at his little girl when she laughed. Then he turned back to Jade and held out the ring. "Will you marry me?"

The ring really had been something he'd been looking for. The smooth oval-shaped jade was surrounded by a dozen diamonds and held on a wide gold band that he knew would look lovely on her finger. The matching band wasn't as wide, but it did have all their initials inside the band, including Angie's. He looked at Jade's face and saw that she was crying.

"It's beautiful. And I'm not going to ask you if you're sure. You must be if you went to all this trouble." He slipped it on her finger and it fit just like he knew it would. "I love you, Quentin."

"And I love you as well. You're the best thing that's ever happened to me." She nodded and pulled Angie in for a hug. "We'll get married as soon as this can be arranged."

Quentin sat on the couch next to Jade and Angie as Blair talked about some of the precautions he'd been working on to keep the family safe. He'd taken his advice and hired a few body guards, as well as armed a few of the wolves that worked the property at nights. Blair was very good at being an alpha of this family, and Quentin was proud to be a part of it.

"And I have an announcement to make as well." Blair stood up and pulled Sapphire with him. "We're going to have a baby. I'm sure most of you know already, but we wanted to have a little time to ourselves about this, so we sort of kept it to ourselves. It's...you've no idea how happy I am."

Quentin laughed when everyone pulled gifts from every corner of the room and presented them to the couple. Even Angie had one that she laid on the top of the growing pile. When she stared at Sapphire for several seconds, she finally spoke in a low frightened voice.

"Uncle Roger said that girls would whip their babies. You won't do that, will you, Aunt Sapphire? You won't whip them, will you? Even if they're bad?"

Sapphire pulled her into her lap. "Did he say whip or whelp, honey? Because there is a big difference."

Angie seemed to consider it and frowned, then looked at him. He could see her mind working through it, and when she smiled, he knew that she'd gotten it worked out. "He said whelp. I thought he was saying something mean, but that's not mean, is it?"

"No, Angie, it's what our kind does when we have children. We whelp them." Sapphire looked at him before continuing. "She is aware of what we are, right?"

"Oh, I know what you are. You're a wolf like my uncle. But you're not really. He's big and scary and comes into my room when he watches me, with Debra, and he turns into a wolf and snaps at me if I don't do what he says." Quentin started toward her when Jade stopped him. Angie didn't seem to think what she was saying was all that bad. "One night he came in the room and said if I told Daddy he was there he'd come back and tear my arms off and eat them. But I locked my door after that. Then Jade came along, and I didn't have to be watched by him again."

Quentin was going to kill his brother.

Chapter 11

Roger moved a good deal slower than he did before being shot, but he was feeling better daily. He was just sitting at the table thinking about the dream he'd had about Debra and the strange feelings he had about her being dead. When someone knocked on his door, he moved toward it only to have it explode open, and a man holding his dad about a foot from the floor came in. He was holding his dad like he weighed nothing.

"What do you want?" The man dropped his dad, who lay there without moving for several minutes. When he started coughing, Roger looked at the vampire who dared hurt what was his.

"Sit." The man raised a brow at him when Roger only stood there. "This will go a good deal better for you if I don't have to hurt you, too. I've wasted enough time just trying to find you. I won't let you help me get to your brother if you don't simply fucking do as I tell you."

Roger helped his dad up first. Then when he had a drink of water and was sitting, so did he. The man might be this bad assed vampire, but this was Roger's home and—

"How the hell did you get in here? I didn't invite you." He nodded toward his father. "This is my place, not his."

"But he doesn't feel that way. Are we going to have to have a fight about how I can do pretty much whatever the fuck I want, or are you going to shut the fuck up and listen? I don't have all night you know."

If it was supposed to be a joke, Roger didn't think it was all that funny. His father was wincing every time he swallowed, and this asshole had yet to do anything more than piss him off. He glared at him.

"I'm Kent Ballard, or at least that's what I go by now." He grinned as he pulled out a chair and straddled it from behind. "You know Jade Erickson. She is the fucking cunt you're going to help me get."

"Why? Debra is the one you have to talk to about her. She hates the girl." Roger thought again about the dream he'd had and wondered briefly if she was all right. "Have you talked with my mate?"

"Oh yeah, we did a little talking before I made a nice meal of her and her lovely body." Roger started to stand but was frozen in place. "You'll sit down or I won't tell you what a fine piece of ass she was."

Roger fought it but in the end had to sit. Draining his strength fighting this bastard now wasn't going to help him if he attacked them. Roger asked him what he knew about his Debra.

"Your Debra? I think not. At least not when she came to me. She said you scammed her about a house you left a dead body in. One she was sure you'd fucked." He winked at him. "Not that I blame you on that. Pussy is pussy, right? Anyway, she mentioned that she was pissed at this bitch because she took her man. I'm guessing she wanted him because of his money."

"He's my brother and he's been fucking me over for a long time. Dad too." Which wasn't really the truth—not even close — but what the fuck did it matter now really? "I want him before he and that fucking cunt Erickson whelp a brat and I get nothing."

"You think you should have it all? Well, not going to happen now. I want my part, which isn't going to leave a great deal after I'm finished. I'm very selfish like that." He leaned his chin on his hands that rested on the back of the chair. "I tell you what. If you help me get Jade and all in one piece, I'll let you kill off the brother. I have no use for him, and as far as I can remember, he'll be willing to give up Jade without much of a fight. She's a lousy lay, and I can't stand her."

"But you want her?" Kent nodded and smiled. "I don't understand. If you don't want her for sex or for herself, what the fuck are we doing here?"

"I never said I didn't want to fuck her. I said she was a lousy lay. And let's just say she's the one that got away and I need to rectify that. As soon as possible as a matter of fact." Kent stood up and stretched before continuing. "I want you to find her and bring her here. I'll do the rest. I don't care how you do it, but do it."

"And if we don't? Then what?" Roger wasn't prepared for his quick move. Before he could finish the implied threat, he was lifted up off the chair and dangling from the vampire's hand in seconds. When he pulled him to his throat, Roger had a moment of panic. Then nothing. The last thing he heard before the darkness took him was his father screaming.

~~~

"This is a Fowler's Toad. See how his vent is long? Their dorsal colors are brown, tan, gray, or light green with a series of dark spots along their back to their groin. Their chests are white." Jade pointed to the little girl in the front who raised her hand.

"Where do they live all the time? And how do I help them when I find them?" Typical question for a child, but not usually from a girl. Jade laughed.

"You really shouldn't help them because studies have shown that their numbers sadly are beginning to decline. We need to preserve what few we have left so that our next generations can enjoy them. They're a wild animal like all the other creatures that live out in the woods and surrounding areas. But they can be found most anywhere. They don't mind the open air and can be found not only around rivers and streams, but in barns as well as in your yard."

Each child got to see the small frogs as they sat and honked at them. As they moved deeper into the forest, she saw two wolves running with them, but they never encroached in her area. She knew that they weren't the usual kind of wolves, but ones that would sit down with their families later tonight and watch television afterward. She steered her group to the next area.

By the time her hour with the group of Junior Rangers was finished, she was glad to sit down. They always made her day, younger kids wanting to know just what was going on in the woods behind their home or in the parks, but their endless questions made her head ache. She was still sitting in the lounge when one of the other rangers came in.

"You have a man at the desk that wants to talk to you. He said it's important." Jade nodded and started to stand when the woman continued. "He looks like someone knocked him around a little. Hard to believe that someone would tangle with a guy that big."

Jade paused before standing. She had no idea who it might be but feared it might be Roger. Cautiously, she sniffed the air and found that while there were too many scents in the room to really help her, she still believed it to be Roger.

Moving slowly to the door, she peered around the slightly opened door to see. Still nothing. Taking a deep breath, she moved into the open lobby and saw him standing about ten feet from the door.

"What do you want?" Startling him, he turned to her, and Jade had a moment to wonder if he'd even tried to heal himself. "You're being hunted by all kinds of agencies as well as a few wolves I know, but here you stand. So again I ask you, what the hell do you want?"

"I'm here to take you back with me, but I think there are too many witnesses around for me to try that." She looked around and saw that they were the only two in the room, then looked back at him. "I'm working with a friend of yours, and he seems to think you're the one that got away."

Kent. Her mind screamed at her to run but knew that it was impossible for Kent to be here during the daylight hours. Lifting her chin, she glared at Roger and waited for him to continue. When he didn't, she noticed that he had an envelope in his hands. Almost as soon as she saw it, he dropped it on the floor and nodded at her.

"My father is dead. Your friend said that it was his payment for all the problems you've caused him. I'm not sure what my father had to do with the issues between the two of you, but he's dead all the same." She started to tell him she was sorry for his loss when he cut her off. "He's going to get the brat too and make her like him. I don't like the kid all that much, but I'm thinking she'll make a great monster."

His head shaking was in direct opposition to what he was saying. She had a sudden thought that he was terrified and only doing as he had been directed. When she nodded back at him, he seemed to sag with relief.

"Is De…my mate, is she dead?" She nodded at his very softly spoken question. "Did he…was he responsible?" Again she nodded, and he looked away from her.

"Your brother was with her. She told him who had hurt her." Roger didn't say anything, but she could almost feel his anguish. "Do you need help?"

His laughter was bitter. "I'm beyond that now, I'm afraid. I've no way to escape him or ever be free of him. He's taken what he needed to find me, hear me. If I speak a name, he will come for me. I've…I'm as good as dead."

Jade almost felt sorry for him. He was going to die. And while she didn't care for the man, he was still her future brother-in-law. When he turned back, he nodded toward the envelope, and she leaned over to pick it up as soon as he turned his back. She had a feeling that what Roger said was true; Kent was able to see what he did and said, so she quickly hid it behind her.

"I'll be back for you. Mark my words that when I come, I'm going to take you to him. It's out of my hands." She nodded at his back and then told him she'd be waiting for him. "Convert him."

Roger walked out the door before she could ask him what he meant. When he was out of her sight, she pulled the envelope out of her back pocket and looked at the front. It was addressed to Quentin. Going to the back room, she gathered up her things and headed for the door. She was in the parking lot when her cell phone rang, startling a small scream from her.

"I wanted to know if you'd like to get dinner in town. Angie is staying at your sister's house, and we have a free night. I've rented us a room." She felt her body respond to Quentin's sexy voice, but it was overridden by fear. "There are so many things I want to do to you. First of which is drink from your pussy. I've not had a lot of time at that one feast."

"I need to see you now." He laughed. "I have something for you. Something that will...Roger was here today."

The change in his voice was immediate. "When? Did he hurt you? I'm coming there right now. Stay inside and wait for me."

"He gave me a message for you. Roger also said your father was dead." She could hear a sharp intake of his breath and her heart broke for him. "I'm so sorry."

"I'm coming to you. Could you please stay there until I get there?" She told him she would. "I'm going to contact Sloan. I'd like...I'd very much like you to consider doing what he asked. I know it's going to be hard for you and I'd like to think I can protect you at all costs, but I'm thinking I can't. Not as a human." She heard a car door shut and wondered if he'd drive while this upset when he answered her unspoken question. "When the driver pulls up, I'll come inside to get you. Please, just stay where there are people."

Jade moved back into the building and to the break room. "I'm so sorry about this. I think...Roger said that I should convert you. It was his last words to me before he left."

"I believe he's correct, don't you? I will be stronger too...fuck, I don't know what I can do, but being able to be as strong as you will at least give me a fighting chance." She agreed with him. "I'm in love with you, Jade. So much so that my heart aches to think that you're in danger."

"We're both in danger. And we have to protect Angie, too. Roger mentioned that Kent was going to hurt her as well." She heard him cursing and knew just how he felt. "We'll do everything to protect her, Quentin. I swear to you that nothing will happen to her."

"I know you'll try, but I'm still scared out of my mind to let her out of my sight." She heard him tell the driver something. "I'm going to be there in ten minutes. I think we should go back to the house and try to work this out. I want this over with, don't you?"

"More than you can think." She sat down on the small couch and tried to think after hanging up with Quentin. He said he wanted to contact Blair as well as Donny. The man was going to be following her everywhere now; she just knew it. When Quentin came into the small break room, she was still seated and he pulled her up from the couch only to pull her tightly against his body.

"I love you." She nodded and let him hold her, loving the feeling of him so close. "I've contacted Sloan. I know you never answered me, but I have to at least try and protect you both. You're all I—"

"I agree. I'll let him bite me." She shivered and Quentin pulled her tighter against him as she thought of fangs biting into her flesh. "I also think it would be smart of us to have him do the same to Angie like you said. Kent will go for her and he'll hurt her if we…Quentin, Roger said that Kent was going to change her into a vampire. If he does, she'll never grow up."

"He'll touch her over my dead body." Not words that made her feel good, and she told him so. "I'm sorry, love, but I can't stand the thought of this prick doing anything at all to you or our daughter."

Her heart blossomed when he called Angie her daughter, too. She already loved the little girl like her own and wanted to protect her as well. She let him snuggle into her neck, knowing that he'd find as much comfort there as she did when he touched her.

"How do we do the change?" She let his question float over her, trying to think of a way to lock the door and have him naked at the same time. "Jade?"

"I want you." He licked the pulse at her throat, and she moaned. "You're not helping me. I have to go out into the lobby and into your car before we can get home so you can fuck me."

"Or I can give you what you need in the limo, then take you home and we can play on the bed." She moaned when he cupped her ass, bringing her flush against his erection. "You have any idea how badly I want to lean you over this couch and fuck you?"

"Yes," she hissed at him as he rocked into her harder. "Quentin, we can't do this here. Any number of people are going to come into the room soon, and we're going to get caught."

"Then we have to hurry." Taking her hand, he led her out to the waiting limo and helped her into the back seat. She wasn't even completely on the seat before he had her lying down on the seat and was pulling her pants off. Christ, she was going to come just from the anticipation.

As soon as her pants were discarded to the floor, he was kneeling down on the carpet and pulling her to him. She felt her pussy float with desire. And when he licked her from gate to clit, she nearly screamed.

"You're going to have to be quiet, baby. Our driver is old, but I'm betting he could hear you scream when you came if you do it like I love." She nodded, not really caring if the entire world heard her right now. "If you be quiet when you come, I'll let you scream your head off when I take you on our new bed."

"I don't know if I can." She moaned when he pressed a finger into her sheath. "Quentin, please don't tease me. I need this."

"As do I." He licked her again, then suckled her clit into his mouth and nipped before lifting his head. Her entire body was on fire, and she needed some relief right now. Curling her fingers into his hair, she pulled him back to her pussy and held him there. When he suckled on her clit again, she nearly cried out, but didn't want to know what he'd do if she didn't do as he asked.

Jade came twice before they were out of the city. And when she reached for her service pants, he pulled them from her and pulled her over his naked cock. She rode him slowly at first until he freed her breast and pulled her nipple into his mouth.

"I want you to start the change now." She nodded but only continued to take a slow ride over his cock. When he stopped her with his fists at her hips, she looked at him.

"You're sure about this?" He nodded. "Blair has given me permission, but I need you to say the words to him. I'm not going to have someone say that you were forced because of the things going on right now."

"I would never say that and I've already spoken to Blair. He said for you to do it and he'd be there if you needed him." Quentin kissed her throat, and she threw back her head to give it all to him. "He told me that it would be painful but that I was healthy enough that I could take it."

"You'll be sore for a few days." He sat up and she felt his cock throbbing deep inside of her. "Quentin, you're going to make me come if you continue to do that."

"Do it, Jade. Make me yours." Her canines dropped suddenly, and she felt her wolf move along her skin. When Quentin bared his throat for them both, she and her wolf leaned in and licked him. As soon as he rolled her to her back and began pounding hard into her, she let her wolf come out to mark him, and she growled low as she sank her canines into him.

Quentin cried out, but she was sure it was from his release rather than any pain she might have caused him. By the time she came, screaming, he was well on his way to becoming a wolf like her.

Chapter 12

Kent watched the wolf as he paced. He wasn't aware of him yet, but that was because Kent didn't want him to be, not because the man wasn't paying attention to his surroundings. When he stopped suddenly and looked at the door, Kent moved deeper into his shadows and waited for whatever came through the door before he moved in any direction.

The woman who came in seemed to know Witt, but not well. She nodded to him once and hugged him to her. When she left again, Kent had a moment to wonder if Witt was going with her, but he only sat down in the chair and closed his eyes. He sat that way for perhaps five minutes before Kent heard him snore loudly. He went to him and kicked him in the feet to wake him.

"You have time to sleep now, wolf? What of the assignment that I gave you? Have you located the woman?" He nodded but didn't rise. For a reason that Kent could only think was arrogance, Witt laid his head back and closed his eyes again. Another kick to his legs this time had him sitting up.

"What?" It took Kent several minutes to get his temper back under control when Witt continued to stare at him before the wolf spoke again. "I'm working on it. I've feelers out, and the fact that she's got several body guards around her at all times is not making my job any easier. Did you know that they're looking for you?"

Kent hadn't realized that she knew he was coming for her, but then he'd not heard all that the fucking bitch of a human had told before he felt her. Killing the human that Witt called Debra had been a mistake, he'd admit that now, but she'd pissed him off. Firstly, because she was not where he'd told her to be, which was in his bed. And secondly because she'd been telling them about him and what he'd planned. Which he'd strictly forbidden her to do. Humans were so unreliable.

"Whatever reason do they have to be searching for me? Unless it is because you told them of me." He waited for the wolf to say something, but he only stared at him. Kent moved into his mind and could see where he'd talked to Jade, but he'd not taken her. There had been too many people around. Like he cared about whether or not the wolf would have been caught.

"If they would have caught me with her, you'd never get her." Soundly put, but Kent didn't have to like it. He sat down in the chair across from Witt and moved into his mind again. He didn't care if he hurt him, but he had information that he wanted.

"She comes and goes without thought to me getting her, I see." Witt nodded but still didn't move off the couch. There was something wrong with him, and it took him several minutes to figure it out. The wolf was dying.

"I have a plan to pick her up in the morning. Once I have her…once she's here, you'll let me go, right?" Kent didn't answer him but continued to think how the wolf could be dying. "I want to go and try to rest for a while. I don't…I haven't been myself lately."

"You're dying." Witt nodded and leaned his head back against the couch again, closing his eyes. "What happened to you? Drugs? Heart? I thought you were in perfect health if you shifted."

"I don't know what's wrong with me." Kent raped his mind and was angry with himself when he did it gently. But he needed the wolf, he told himself, and didn't want him to die before he had Jade. He only found that the man was dying, and he honestly didn't know why. There was something there, but Witt spoke before he could chase it down.

"I'll have her here when you rise next. You can count on that." Witt lay his head back and it tilted to the right. Kent's hunger spiked at that moment and he wanted to bite the wolf and taste of him. When he stood up, he heard the lure of his blood moving through his body and leaned over the sleeping man. Sinking his fangs, he drank deeply.

He'd only taken a few hard pulls on the man when he felt the first tingling of fear. He at first thought it to be Witt's, but soon he realized it was his own. Staggering back from him, Kent sat on the couch again and felt the blood rush through him like a drug. Then the pain struck him. Christ, he was doubling over with it. It wasn't long before Kent was on the floor and in a great deal of pain. He looked up at Witt when he realized he was awake.

"It's silver. I knew you'd drink from me again and I had someone put a spell over me so that you'd not be able to tell until it was too late." Witt stood up and staggered slightly before falling back to his seat. "Of course I knew that someone as powerful as you claim to be would need more than I had in me originally, so she had me drink a little more. It'll kill me quicker, but I was going to die anyway."

"You poisoned me?" Witt laughed and nodded. "What the hell for? What the fuck did I do to you but offer you everything you ever wanted?"

Which wasn't true. The only thing he'd given the wolf was orders and a lie that he'd give him his brother when this was over. Another cramp hit his belly, and Kent doubled over in pain. Witt laid his head back, and Kent realized that he'd never sealed the wound at his throat. Standing as best he could, mostly leaning on the couch and anything else that was close, he moved up to the wolf and sank his teeth into him again, this time careful not to drink, and tore his throat out. When Kent leaned back to watch the man drain out, he was startled to see a smile on his face.

"Thank you." Kent wasn't sure he'd heard him correctly and started to ask him what he'd said. But he continued talking in a much lower voice. "She's going to kill you now, and I hope that she makes it slowly. Jade will tear you apart, and I can die happily knowing that I saved them all from you."

Kent lay on the floor and tried to think while Witt took his last breaths. He had to find someone to drink from, someone with untainted blood. A faerie would do nicely, but the only one he knew wasn't speaking to him at the moment. He smiled at the memory before he realized he needed fresh blood. Standing again, he moved to the door and went out into the hall. There he found a woman just putting trash in a cart, and pulled her to his mouth before she could scream. It helped, but it wasn't enough.

There were two more women on the floor he was on, and he killed both before he felt his strength returning. He was going to have to find shelter soon, something underground to heal, but he knew it was going to be a long time before he could rise without feeling the effects of the silver, if he ever got over it. When he went into the night, he found three more victims, but none of them what he really needed. But going to ground was not an option. He moved through the night and killed five more people before he took shelter in a cave miles from the wolf and his prey. Kent was going to have to lay low for at least a few days. And when he came out, he was going to find Jade and her family and feast on them all for what they'd done to him.

It was nearly sunrise when he finally felt the pain recede enough that he could rest. He'd been in a great deal of pain for most of the night. And now that he could rest, he began to feel his anger surge forward.

"The fucking cunt is responsible for this." Kent tried to think through the haze of pain who he was thinking about, and Jade popped into his mind. "I should have killed her when she tried to leave me. I will know better next time."

He laughed slightly but winced at the pain it caused him. When he rolled to his back, he felt the silver race through his veins and wanted to find the wolf and kill him again. The fucking bastard had actually tried to kill him. "What an ungrateful bastard. And to think I was going to let him…he would have been able to kill that fucking bastard of a brother if he'd only done what I'd ordered him to."

Kent laid there for several more minutes, the sun pulling at him hard now. He knew that he had to rest, but his mind would hardly let him. The man had poisoned him. What the hell had he done that for? Kent was a powerful vampire, and now he'd been reduced to hiding out until his body could heal properly. When rest claimed him, his mind was still working on the whys of it all. He would be better equipped to reason it when he rose, he thought, and closed his eyes.

~~~

Quentin opened his eyes and quickly closed them again. The pain of the light sent sword-like pain through his head. And he could swear he heard his hair growing.

"You'll learn to tone it down." He knew that Blair spoke softly, but his voice still sounded as if he'd shouted right next to his ear. "How are you feeling otherwise?"

Quentin took a quick inventory of his body. He was sore in so many places that he felt as if he'd been in an accident but had come out okay. Opening his eyes again, he looked at Blair, thankful that he'd turned off the lights.

"I hurt. Am I supposed to?" Blair shrugged. Quentin had a feeling that the man was relieved about something, but was not sure what it was. As he sat up on the bed, he noticed that he was in the clinic and not home like he'd started out.

"There were complications. You had to be brought here or die. It was nothing that Jade did, but something about your background that had us...did you know that somewhere in your line there is a panther?"

"No." He tried to reason around that but he hurt a great deal more now that he was sitting up. "What would that have to do with me becoming a wolf?"

"A wolf is a canine, and a panther is not." Understanding started to filter through his head as the haze of pain started to shift away. "When she started the change, you were fine, if you remember. Then something started to shift. You're not wholly human. Just enough of the cat came to the surface that he started to get pissed off when the wolf started to show. She had you brought here. I had to...she was resting."

"How long have I been here?" Blair looked at the door, and when it opened, Quentin felt as if his world righted and the pain completely disappeared. There stood Jade. When she came to his bedside and touched him, Quentin felt something inside of him stir.

"You okay?" He nodded and pulled her down for a kiss. Hunger blasted through him, and he pulled her over him just as he heard the door click again. Not caring if someone came in or Blair left them, he rocked up into her softness as she moaned.

"I want you." She nodded and pulled at the gown he had on. When she bit into his shoulder just enough to cause him a touch of pain, he snarled. The sound was so startling to him he stopped pulling her clothes off.

"Did I do that?" Smiling, she nodded at him. "That felt...amazing. Like it came from deep inside of me."

"I think it was your wolf." She shifted on the bed so that she was sitting over his lap, and he couldn't help but pull her over him in a riding motion. "He's very aggressive, but the cat will be, too, when he finds his ground."

Quentin was barely paying attention to her when she leaned down and licked his throat. But she'd said cat, too, and he pulled her up and looked at her.

"What do you mean, 'when he finds his ground'? I'm wolf, right?" She nodded, then shook her head. "Jade? What the hell happened to me?"

She got off him and then the bed. When she started to pace, he started to feel his entire world start to splinter into pieces as parts of his memory from the past...was it a few days or just one? Anyway, he remembered her screaming when he'd clawed at her. Sloan was there and yelling at him to drink. Then he'd shifted. But into what?

"You're both a cat and a wolf. I'm not sure how that works for you, but you are both. Sloan said that somewhere in your linage you had a full-blooded panther in your family, and it's lain dormant for all this time. Up until I tried to convert you into a wolf. He...your cat, didn't much care for that."

"I hurt you." She nodded but didn't say anything. "Come here, Jade, and let me look at it. I want to see how badly I hurt you."

"I'm going to be fine. It'll heal once I shift, but I was afraid to do it in the event you needed me. I've been...Blair put me into a sleep yesterday and now I feel a good deal better." He told her again to come to him. "Seriously, Quentin, I'm fine."

"Then show me." He realized that he was feeling her fear, and his animal, whichever it was, started to feed on it. Quentin felt something run along his arm and looked down to see fur sprouting there, and he looked at Jade.

"It's your wolf. Let him come and you'll shift." Nodding, he closed his eyes and waited. When nothing appeared to be happening, he opened them and had to blink several times before he could focus. "You're beautiful."

Quentin opened his mouth to tell her that nothing worked when a growl spilled from his lips. Looking down at what he thought would be his arms, he saw furred appendages that he assumed belonged to him. When he growled again this time, he felt powerful and leapt from the bed to go to this mate.

"You did that very well. Like you knew just what you were doing." He rubbed his head along her leg and bumped his head against her until she moved to the chair. She sat down and ran her fingers deep into his head just behind his ears. "You're very dark. Almost a blue-black. Probably because of your cat. Your fur is softer, too, slick feeling under my fingers."

He purred. It came from deep within his chest and out his mouth. Something he'd never thought of a wolf doing, but again, he wasn't a normal wolf. When he closed his eyes, Quentin saw him there. The panther was just pacing back and forth as if he was awaiting his turn for something. When he snarled at him, Quentin laughed. He'd never felt so good in his entire life.

"Can we talk like this?" Jade told him that they could. "I wonder if the panther will be able to talk to you as well. I can see him. Just there beyond my mind. He's huge. Am I that big as a wolf?"

"You are. Bigger than me but not as big as Blair, but not much difference. Maybe thirty pounds or less. You're darker than he is, shiny in your coat as I said, but you're...I don't know, you seem more powerful to me. Could be that I'm thinking that now because you're in front of me."

"I'm much bigger, and we'll leave it at that." She laughed again, and he felt happy. "How do I shift back? And just so you know, I'm still going to see how I hurt you."

"You clawed me when your panther came to surface. He didn't mean to, but I was in his way when you wanted to run. I won't do it again. Blair had to...he held you down and had to order you to shift back. You terrified us all." He moved back from her lap and thought of himself. But the panther leapt to his mind at the last moment, and he knew when he opened his eyes that he wasn't wolf or human right now.

His cat snarled, and he could feel his anger. When he moved to Jade, she backed deep into the chair, but she didn't run. Much to his disappointment. But he wanted something from her and when he nudged at her shirt, she tried to pull away. That's when Quentin realized he wanted to see the wound, too.

"Show us what he did. He wants to see it." She shook her head, and that pissed the cat off. "Do it, Jade, please? He really needs to see what he did."

When she stood up, Quentin sat down and tried to calm his cat by telling him that she was doing what he wanted. He was still very angry, but he did it calmly now and not aggressively. When Jade pulled her blouse off and held it in front of her like a shield, the cat reached up and pulled it away gently, using his claws to do so.

The marks were long and jagged. Four wide red wounds marred her lovely flesh, and he started to whimper. The cat was so upset that he'd harmed his mate that Quentin almost felt sorry for him. Moving forward, Quentin had the sudden urge to lick the wounds and taste her blood. There was no talking him out of it. And when he pushed her back into the chair, Jade tried to cover herself again.

"Let him lick them. He wants to…I think he wants to heal you." Jade nodded and lowered her hands. "Jade, honey, I'm so sorry."

"You didn't do anything. You were hurt and scared. I was in the wrong place at the wrong time." Quentin wasn't sure that was right, but when the cat put its paws on either side of her on the chair, she leaned back and let him look at the wounds.

They were infected. He could smell that now, and he leaned closer and sniffed. Yes, that was what he smelled. Somehow she'd gotten an infection from his marks. He looked into her eyes as he lapped at her too-warm flesh. Her moan made his wolf stir.

"They want you. So do I, but I'm not sure how this works." He licked the path of the wounds again and again until he felt that she'd heal now. "When I shift, you should know that I'm going to take you. Right here and right now."

"I hope so." She stood up and removed her bra. "Shift for me, Quentin. I need you very badly."

But he didn't. He watched her until she was naked before him, and he moved to her, not sure what his cat was going to do, but he rubbed his head along her thigh, then backed up.

He'd just marked her if he was thinking correctly. Closing his eyes, Quentin reached for himself and felt the power of his shift take him. When he opened his eyes, he was no longer looking up at her but down on her as Quentin.

"Come here." She went into his arms willingly, and he took her mouth. Knowing that he wasn't going to be gentle, he picked her up and impaled her over his cock. Nothing had ever felt this good as to be deep inside of his mate. When he took her to the wall, he pounded into her hard enough to shake pictures from their hangers and make the curtain move. When he felt her lick along his throat, Quentin snarled at her and she growled low. He was going to take her throat this time and mark his mate.

The wolf surfaced then, just enough that Quentin felt his canines drop. When he tore into her flesh, Jade screamed out his name and he came with her. Even as his body was filling hers he felt the need to take her again. Letting her go as soon as her feet were on the floor, he turned her and pulled her ass to him. Entering her from behind, he bit into her shoulder again and tasted her hot spicy blood fill his mouth.

"Come now," he commanded her and pinched her clit with his finger and thumb. *"Come, Jade. Come now."*

Her body tightened around his and he found himself strangled inside of her. She pulled his arm to her mouth and bit hard into his forearm even as he came. Christ, he couldn't get enough of her. Wasn't sure he ever wanted to. When they both leaned heavily against the door, panting, he felt his cock stir to life again, and he chuckled.

"I have never gone three times before even as a teenager in the blossom of my youth." He rocked into her again, and she moaned. "We really should try this in a bed. I'm sure that would more than likely be more comfortable than the wall."

"Or the woods." Quentin was licking her shoulder clean of her blood when she suggested that. He felt his wolf and the cat perk up, and Jade lifted her head to look at him over her shoulder. "You want to take me like a wolf, don't you?"

"Yes. More than anything in this world." He backed away from her, but only far enough that he could turn her around before pressing her back. "Will you shift for me and let me fuck you like an animal?"

"Oh hell yeah." She pushed him back and moved to her clothes. "As soon as we get home, we'll go to the woods behind your house and run through the woods."

Quentin pushed her over the bed while she was reaching for her blouse. An urge to dominate her made his wolf snarl at him to take her again. When she opened her legs for him, he slammed into her heat and stilled.

"Our home. Say it. It's our home." She moaned and he pulled out to the tip then slammed deeper into her. The bed moved across the floor a good foot, and he had to take a step to lean over her. "Say it, Jade. Say it's our home."

"Our home. Christ, Quentin, give it to me. I need to come again." Happy to oblige, he reached around her to her slick pussy and found her clit. She was as hard as he was, and he slid his fingers over her gently as he moved in and out of her much slower now.

"When we get home, I'm going to make you come so many times you're going to need a nap just to make it back to our bed. Then when you're there, I'm going to take you again and again." He had no idea if he could actually do that to her, but he was willing to try. "Then when you're sated, I'm going to hold you for the rest of the night until I need you again."

"Please," she begged him, riding his fingers. "I need to come. Please give it to me." He nipped at her shoulder again and tasted her need. Quentin moved into her mind and found that he could see what she wanted, and stood up. Pulling from her body was the hardest thing he'd ever done, but he wanted to give her as much pleasure as she'd given him. Helping her to stand, he told her to lie back on the bed.

He slid the chair to the side of the bed and then pulled her to the very edge and put her foot into his hand. As he massaged it, he smiled at her. She was going to enjoy this. And so was he. Leaning into her, he licked her thigh and growled low when she tried to close her legs to him.

"Don't deny us this." He felt his wolf stir, and he tried to hold him back. But when he snarled at him too, he let him come to the surface just a little. His wolf wanted to taste her too.

Suckling her clit into his mouth, Quentin let the wolf have his way. He never fully shifted, but he knew the moment his tongue entered Jade that she could feel the difference, too. She screamed out her first climax almost immediately. Pulling her nether lips open wider, Quentin feasted on her as if she were the last meal he'd ever have. And she fed him all of her. Over and over she came until she started to beg him to stop please.

"I need you." He stood up and fisted his cock. "Christ, I need to come inside of you again."

She reached for him just as he entered her slowly. Every inch of his cock felt bathed in molten lava. When he was buried to the root he leaned over her and took her mouth in a gentle kiss.

"I love you. More than I ever dreamed possible to love someone." He rocked into her over and over, watching her face as he did so. "I want to see you large with my child. I want to wake next to you every day for the rest of my life. I want to be with you every minute of every day."

"Please." He moved a little more now, deeper into her, and he held her tightly to him. "I want to have your child. Soon. I want to have a child with you, as many as we can."

"Will you adopt Angie? Make her yours?" She nodded and closed her eyes. "Let me see you when you come. I want to see it take you."

Opening her eyes, he could see her wolf there and his own stirred against his skin. When she screamed this time, it wasn't his name she yelled out but her love for him. When her teeth sank into his shoulder, he did the same to her. And rolling through his climax, he marked her deeply this time, tearing into her tender flesh and leaving his mark for all to see.

Chapter 13

Sloan sat on the porch and watched the young couple get out of the large SUV. He smiled when he saw Angie try to help her dad move to the house, knowing that the man was much stronger than he looked. And a good deal more than anyone knew. Sloan watched Jade as she pulled the last of the luggage from the back and put it on the ground before closing the door. He was next to her lifting the burden before she could take the handle.

"You're well?" She nodded, not looking him in the face. When he lifted her chin, he could see that she, too, had taken on a little more, but wondered if she knew it yet. This couple had a lot going on.

"You should really step away from her. I'm not sure, but I think one or both of my animals wants to kill you right now." Sloan dropped his hand from Jade and turned slowly to look at Quentin. "You've no idea how much I want to shift and tear you apart."

"I don't know, but I can feel it. You're well also then?" Quentin nodded at his question. "Good. I have news to tell you, and I'd like to—"

He was suddenly pulled into a hard hug. He and Quentin had hugged before, but this one was different. This one was filled with love and understanding. Sloan held his friend as long as he could and they both parted before they got too weird.

"You saved my life." Sloan started to deny it, but Quentin cut him off. "No, you did. Jade told me what you did for us, and I don't know how I'll ever repay you. If you hadn't done what...if you hadn't come when she needed you, we both know that I'd be dead."

"You're welcome. And I would very much appreciate it if you never brought it up again. Even as old as I am and as worldly, I have never been so terrified of anything in my entire life. I've never...." Sloan shivered. "I was glad to help you when I could. That's enough said on that subject."

Quentin nodded and moved to the house with his daughter. Sloan's memories of that night flooded his mind, and he had to hang onto the side of the car to wait for the fear to pass again. He looked at Jade when she put her hand out to him.

"I never thanked you either." He nodded and watched her. "When he started to shift into both animals at the same time, I felt my mind shut down. He was coming apart with them, and there was nothing I could...you saved us both, not just him."

"He was dying. He was as good as dead." He took her hand and held it as they both moved to the house. "I'm happy that—"

Sloan dropped the luggage that was Angie's and pulled Jade into his arms. He knew that if Quentin were out there with them, he'd be hard pressed not to murder him, but he wanted to hold this woman. Not sexually, though she was very beautiful, but because she'd been the lifeline that pulled them all together when the need arose. She'd called to him even though they'd never as much as exchanged anything but scents.

Pulling away from her, he followed her to the house and waited outside the door until she came back for him. The ward he'd had put on the house prevented him from entering, too. Without both their permission, he could neither enter nor leave. It was the way he'd had it set up.

After they were all in the house and Angie was settled in her new room, the adults adjourned to the living room. Sloan loved the furniture that was in this room as well as the rest of the house. When a fire was lit in the big fireplace, the room took on a glow that was only outshined by the two people he had to break hard news to.

"Roger is dead." He had always had an understanding with Quentin that it was hard and fast news, not bits and pieces. Quentin looked shocked but didn't say anything. "His body was found two days ago. I didn't become aware of it until someone from the force called me and told me he had a death he couldn't explain. He'd had his throat torn out."

"By who?" Sloan looked at Jade when she asked. "Was it Kent? Or are there more players that we aren't aware of?"

"It was him. He's also either gone to ground or hurting like hell right now, too. Roger had quite a bit of silver in his system and when Ballard bit him, he would have had to have gotten a good deal of it in his own body. There was a lethal dose in him, much more than would have come from the bullet." Sloan handed them a picture. "Do either of you know this woman?"

"I do." Jade handed the photo to Quentin as she continued. "She's a faerie that I run with sometimes when we're in the woods at the forestry. She's...she can shift to other animals."

Sloan nodded. "Her scent was all over Roger too. I'm thinking she gave him the silver and he took it willingly. He might have even arranged for her to give it to him. It might have been his plan to have Ballard bite him and drink the tainted blood."

"The letter." Quentin jumped up off the couch and went out of the room. When he returned, he had an envelope in his hands and he looked embarrassed. "My brother gave this to me through Jade a few days before I got...before the change. I never read it because I was sure he was going to be asking me for more money or something more than I wanted to give him."

He tore it open and three things fell out to the floor as he took the letter in his hand. Even from across the room he could see that two were pictures and the other looked to be a claim ticket or something. Quentin started to read the letter aloud.

My dearest brother,

You've no idea how sorry I am for all the things I did to you and your family. I know that you've no reason to forgive me, and I'm not asking that of you. But I would, if you'd allow me to, tell you all that I have done. A sort of confession if you like.

I killed Isabel. She had been hanging from the chair that Dad had put her on to teach you a lesson, but I kicked it from her when I went to see her. She'd been begging me to let her down, and I'd been just fired from my latest fuck up, and I was pissed at you for having it all. I never hurt Angie then, but I have since. The child never told on me because I threatened her.

I was cruel to her, Angie I mean. She was nothing but a child. I realize that now, but I hated her because again she was something you had but I did not. I hope that someday she will forget me. It is the only thing I am clinging to right now, that she will have a better life with you and Jade.

Also I was responsible for Debra's deceit. I knew she was my mate long before she met you, but I wanted more, and she did as well. I will say that she was just as devious as I in all manner of things. And for the most part was willing in all the things we did to you, quite happily as a matter of fact. It was our plan, as you had guessed, to get her pregnant with your child then have her divorce you later and live off your checks monthly. You're a good deal smarter than I ever thought. Or for that matter gave you credit for. I'm truly sorry for that.

Kent Ballard will try to kill you. I have hopes that Jade will convert you to wolf before he comes for you. You're very intelligent but not as strong as a vampire. Especially one as old as Kent is. He's sick in the mind, I believe, and thinks himself very much king of the world. He will more than likely kill me in the next few days. My only hope is that I can get this letter to you somehow before then.

He will change Angie if he finds her. You must protect her at all costs. I'm not sure if you realize what that would mean for her to be changed as a child, but she will remain one until her death. As I have done some research on the matter, children who are converted become bigger monsters than their sire. It's because they are not ever an adult and cannot deal with things as we do. Not that I did a very good job at dealing either.

Kent has two lairs. One is in a house that is on Richardson Avenue. The house number eludes me now, but it is a large mansion that sets back from the road a bit. There are two brick and stone columns on the front drive that lead back to the house. He sleeps in the lower levels and had the house wired for intruders. I have taken the liberty of cutting those wires in a way that he is not aware of. When entering the house go to the library, and under the desk is a button. By pushing it, you'll open the doors to the lower levels and to the several lairs below. His is at the end of the long hall. There is no other way in or out of the rooms but by the hall. Take Sloan with you. He'll be able to help you like no one else can.

Sloan cleared his throat, and Quentin looked up at him before continuing on with the letter. "I cannot go with you unless the house belongs to someone besides him. Or I get the approval of someone with authority. Like the alpha who has been hurt or one of his pack who has been hurt by Ballard."

"I'll contact Blair now. I'm sure that when Kent hurt me should be enough, don't you?" Sloan nodded and smiled. It was the first time he'd heard Jade say Ballard's name without cringing. "I'm going with you, too. I want to make sure the bastard is dead before I can move on."

Sloan nodded, knowing that she'd already moved on, but knew that she needed this as well. He leaned back as Quentin picked up the letter where he'd left off.

The second lair he has is a cave deep within the mountains of the state park where Jade works. I don't think he's had it long, but I know that he's been there several times over the past month. I found it funny that all the time he was staying there he'd never found Jade out working. It was a private joke of mine for several days now, and will keep me on the steady course for what I must do to help you. I must kill myself in order to help you.

I have contacted a good friend of Jade's. She wasn't willing to help me at first, but when I explained to her what I wanted, she was more than willing. I have had her give me something that would hasten my death, and also if all goes well, harm if not kill Ballard for you. I will drink the silver into my body, and he will drink from me. I will be in with him when he rises.

I'm truly sorry for all that I've done to you both. I'd like to say that if I could do it all over, I'd be different, but we both know that I wouldn't. I'm just a horrible person and much too much like Dad to have been anything different. Also, I've taken steps to contact Mom. She has agreed to wait until you contact her before she does anything else. I have been remiss by telling her things about you that were never true, and that is why she left you as she did. I do love you, more than I ever thought I could. Your brother, Roger.

Quentin picked up the two pictures and handed them to Jade. She in turn handed them to him. The first one was of Quentin and Roger as children sitting on a porch step, and the next one was of Quentin with his first wife and their new daughter. It looked like they'd only just come home from the hospital. He handed them back to Jade. The last thing was handed to him directly, and he looked at Quentin when he asked him what it was.

"It's a bank safety deposit box receipt. It was opened...." Sloan looked up at the couple. "It was opened five days ago in Jade's name. It's at the National Bank on Tenth Street."

Sloan went to the lower levels just as the sun was coming up. He really didn't need to sleep so early in the morning hours because he was so old, but Angie had gotten up for school and he thought that Jade and Quentin needed some time with her before she left for the day. The guard that he'd planted at the grade school knew that she was to be his number one priority if anything happened, but if need be, he was to try and save all the children should anyone try anything. Angie was as precious to him as she was her parents.

His phone was ringing just as he settled into the bed. Picking it up, he smiled when he realized who it was. Rufus was one of his dearest friends. And also the most ruthless bastard he knew when it came to doing his job.

"Found out something you might want to know. You remember a few years back when we took out that there prick that was a hurting them girl's way down in Mexico?" Sloan winced at his friend's language but knew better than to try and correct him. "You 'member him. He was the guy that was eating them when there was a nice butcher down the road from him."

"Yes, his name was Darren Fisher. You killed him, if I remember correctly, even though we'd been told to bring him in for questioning." Rufus had had no choice but to kill the man, but it was still fun to rib him about it. "If memory serves me, you had to pay a nice tidy fine for it."

"Yeah, but you paid it for me, so it wasn't a total wash. But I'm thinking he had a partner. One that does about the same as he did but a little more...I guess I would call it a little more violent." Sloan sat up in the bed as Rufus continued. "The reason I called you is on account of you and that human you hung out with. What the fuck was his name?"

"I haven't a clue, Rufus. I'm nearly seven thousand years old, and I've been known to hang out with one or two men between now and then." He waited, knowing that it would come to Rufus sooner or later. "Did you ever hear of a panther and a wolf sharing the same man?"

"No. Hell no. You think they fight it out when he's just walking around snarling and snapping at each other?" The laughter was as crude as his language. "You got a punchline with this here joke?"

"No. I've met one. I've known him a while, but he met up with his mate who changed him, and there was a panther linage there with his change. Both reside in the same man. You know him, Quentin Witt. His brother Roger is the one you were—"

"Him, that's him. Not the Witt guy but the other one. Galloway, that one that has all the money and makes them plastic shit that them chicks buy. You still hang with him?" He assured him that he did. "Well, there's his family, you see. Bunch of dames, and from what I heard tell, lookers too. Anyhow…this here partner is looking for the dames. He said that he's going to make him a wall of their more personal parts. Don't know that much right now, but he's thinking one of them is easy pickings."

"Did you find out which one?" Sloan was headed toward the door when he realized he was naked, and walked back to his clothes as he waited on Rufus to answer him. When he didn't after several seconds, Sloan said his name.

"I'm thinking. Damn it all to hell, I had it. If it helps you at all, her name was some sort of jewel." This didn't help really, as all the Erickson women were named after gems. "I think she was something to do with a show of some sorts. Pretty things I'm a thinking."

Opal was the first name that popped into Sloan's head. He'd not met this Erickson because she'd been away on business. Then she was planning a vacation, one that she'd long coveted according to Sapphire. He sat on the bed and tried to think what to do.

"Her name is Opal Erickson, and she's in New Orleans now at a large craft show or something. I want you to go there and find her and stick to her until she returns home. According to her sisters, she's to stop here to drop off her things before she heads to Paris for a month." His friend started cussing, and Sloan smiled. "I'll make it worth your while if you do this for me."

"What?" The suspicion in Rufus's voice had him laugh. "If you're thinking of going through with your threat of sending me to some finishing school, you can fuck off. I like me the way I am."

"As I'm sure all the ladies do as well." Rufus huffed. "I'll help you buy the house you want. I'll even put the down payment on it for you."

Rufus had a problem with money. Not that he spent it all the time. Quite the contrary, he saved it like it was his job. And he had a great deal of it too. But he hated to part with it. Especially when someone else would spend theirs for him. He laughed when Rufus began making noises about insurance and taxes. Sloan waited for him to finish. He'd pay all those if he had the house he wanted and had wanted for nearly a decade. More, if truth be known.

"And you'll not bitch like a little girl if I don't decorate it like one of them fancy magazines you are always looking at?" He probably would, but he told his friend that he wouldn't. "And when I have them girls over, the kind I like, you're not going to turn your nose up at them?"

"You know I will. What fun would we have after all these years together if I didn't give you a hard time about your choice of women? Because more often than not, I'm right about what they want from you." Rufus agreed he'd been right on a couple of them. "What do you say?"

"I'm going. You got a likeness of her? Or something?" He told him no. "Well I guess I could go down there and snoop around. No harm in that is there?"

He knew the Erickson women well enough to know that if Opal caught Rufus snooping around, she'd kick his ass all the way back to Ohio. But instead of telling his longtime friend this, he assured him that it would be fine. Smiling, he told him to be careful.

"You want to tell me why this chickie is so important to Mr. I Don't Need Anyone in My Life?" Rufus laughed. "You no idea what she looks like, so it must be a favor you're working on. Is that it? You want to parlay some good will toward someone?"

"I know her sister. She's a good person. And if you're really good and don't get this girl hurt before she returns here, I'll introduce you to the gems. All six of the women are gems in their own rights." Sloan smiled as he finished telling Rufus. "Both Galloway and Witt are mated to one sister each. You'd better hurry or you'll miss the chance to marry one of them."

"Marry? Are you insane? I'd as soon you cut my dick off and serve it up to me with a skewer. Marry my ass." Rufus went on for several more minutes, and Sloan laughed the entire time. "You might want to take one of them on. You've not had a good lay in what now…two, maybe three thousand years? Your willy still working?"

"My willy is just fine, and I've no desire to have a mate. Not now or anytime in the future. I've had my fill of women clinging to me and wanting things that are best left untouched." Rufus sighed heavily before Sloan continued. "I'll help them out, be their knight in shining armor, but never will I take a mate."

"I hear you. I'm thinking maybe it don't work that way though. I've heard tell that once one of them gets their hooks in you, you're as good as dead meat." He heard his friend laugh nervously. "I'd just as soon meet the sun if one came along for me. Nasty business, them women. You steer clear of them, 'kay?"

After assuring Rufus several times that he would, he went back to the bed. There was nothing he could do today, but he did make a mental note to let Blair know what might be coming. He settled down and wondered if he'd ever meet his mate and hoped that he wouldn't. A man his age was set in his ways and with his luck, he'd be saddled with an Erickson woman and he'd have to murder her the first time she opened her mouth. Of course, if she looked like these woman, he might just make an effort to enjoy her a time or two first. Closing his eyes, he let his sleep claim him. Tonight was going to be a big night for him.

Chapter 14

Kent woke to the sound of water dripping. He wasn't sure where he was at first, but the tick-tick sound of the drip hitting the stone beneath it was something different. Then he remembered that he'd come here to hide. Sitting up slowly, he let his body become accustomed to the night, and then his hunger hit him. Christ, he was starving. Looking at his phone, he realized it had been three days since he'd come here, and his body was weak with the need to feed. Standing up, he moved to the door and stopped when his leg came in contact with a wire. It was tripped before he could think to back off.

Someone had been in his lair. Moving back into the shadows, Kent stood still, waiting for someone or something to come for him. After long minutes, he moved toward the door again, this time careful where he stepped. Before he could take more than a dozen steps, he found another wire, and this one was set with some kind of explosives.

It took him nearly two hours to get out of his cave. There had been over two dozen of the traps set up at different points along the way, and he'd had to unravel them before he could move. Not even levitating out would work. There were some traps as high as the cave ceiling and in such tight places that he'd had no choice but to work through them. When he got out, he took a breath of air and smelled the wolf all over the place, as well as the vampire. When he started forward again, thinking he'd find both bastards, he saw the note waving in the slight breeze. Taking the rock off it, he held it up so that he could read it.

"Congratulations. I wondered if you would make it through our first tests. Sadly, you did, but that's all right. We get the rest of your short life to play this game. Sincerely, Sloan Crane."

"Mother fuck." Kent tossed the note to the ground, only to find another one attached to a tree not far from where he had found the first one. Taking the nail out, he opened this one to find another note from Crane.

"Too bad about you littering. You know that the woods around here are protected. Pick up the paper and do the responsible thing and clean up after yourself." This time it was signed simply "Sloan."

Kent was bending to pick up the trash when he realized what the fuck he was doing and tossed both pieces to the ground. Taking flight in the sky as a bird, he was so pissed off he nearly forgot to look for prey. When he landed in the little town just below the caves, he noticed that everything was closed up tight and there wasn't a person around. He wandered around for nearly an hour looking for anyone and was completely pissed when there wasn't a soul out. Not even a fucking dog.

It was getting later and later and he needed to feed. Going to the next town proved to be just as unfruitful. He was ready to go on when he spied another note. This one was attached to a building that Kent knew. He'd fed from the patrons of this bar several times over the past months, and now it was as if someone had come along and told them about him. Kent yanked the note off and nearly didn't read it, but curiosity got the better of him.

"You must be starved by now. Good. A hungry vampire is an idiot, and we both know that you're an idiot. What sort of person kills where he lives? You apparently. But I digress. You must feed, and I'm betting you want something without the taint of silver this time." Kent felt his blood run cold at the mention of silver. If he could, he'd go and find the fucking wolf and kill him again. "You should know that as you approach each town, the people in it will have the most amazing need to go home, lock their doors, and not let you in. I am quite proud of that little spell, and am glad to see that it's working."

There was a large S this time at the end of the note, but a postscript had been added. "Have you had enough yet? If so, meet me in the alley near the antique shop. You know the place. It's where you left the body of Alan Witt."

Kent roared out his anger. This was going too far. How had the man found out any of this information? And for that matter, where the hell was he? Kent wadded the note up and tossed it in the trash can as he made his way in the opposite direction of the shop. He wasn't going to walk into a trap any more than he would believe that someone had that much control over humans. If that were the case, he'd have heard about it. Kent hadn't lived for over five hundred years without learning a thing or two about magic.

At nearly sunrise, Kent was willing to admit defeat. There wasn't a person to be found anywhere he looked, and the harder he tried to find someone, the more drained he felt. Making his way to his house this time, he nearly wept when there was another note attached to the front door. He jerked the envelope open and tore the note in half. Reading it was difficult, but he finally got it read.

"You should have come to see me. Now we're going to do this the hard way. Your home has been locked from you. As of now, you've nowhere to go. The caves that you rested in so quietly for the last several days will no longer allow you to enter. I've taken steps." Kent threw back his head and screamed. It was primal, and he heard birds leave their nests in fear. As he started reading again, he could feel his anger boil over and his sight marred by the red gleam of his kind. The sun was cresting when he finally read the last part.

"Have you had enough yet? You'll meet me at the shop or I'll continue to starve you one night at a time. I know who you are now, and I'll stop at nothing to bring you to justice. Adam Stein has a great many things to pay for."

He knew his name. Not the name he'd adopted when he'd come to this world, but his given name. The one he'd been born with and had used the first few decades of his new life. And that man, Stein, did indeed have a great deal to pay for. Firstly and most heinously was the murder of his family so many years ago.

Kent had no choice but to go to ground. He hated sleeping beneath the ground almost as much as he hated the man who now tormented him. There were bugs and crawling things there, and he hated them. As soon as the earth settled over him, he tried to think of anything else but where he was, and he thought of the night he'd killed his parents and his sisters and brother.

They'd told him he was no longer welcome into their home. Not that it had been much of a home, but it was the only one he'd ever known. But when he'd told them what he'd done, how he'd become a man who would live forever, they'd closed the door in his face and forbade him entrance. Kent…Adam then…had begged for hours to be let in, and told them of all the things he could provide for them.

"Go away, you monster." His mother had broken his heart with her words and still he tried to reason with her. "You're a monster of the worst kind. Feeding from the bodies of others like a monster that you are. Go away and never return."

The next night he'd gone back to the house and they'd been asleep this time. Garlic had hung from every window and over both doors. He'd tried to cross the threshold but had been unable. His master laughed at him when he'd fallen back after trying to run at it.

"They must invite you in. As you've never felt this was your home, you are unable to enter without permission." Neal, his maker and sometimes friend, nodded to the house. "Why you'd want to enter that hovel is beyond me, but you must ask them to allow. If I were you, I'd kill the lot of them. No parent should be so unaccepting of their own child."

Kent had glared at the house and could think where each of them lay. His parents would be in the smallest of the three bedrooms, and his brother in the larger room he'd shared with him. And his two sisters would be in the kitchen watching the fire all night so that they'd be warm throughout the night.

Neal helped him to bar the doors. The windows were a little harder for him, as there was no glass, but they'd managed to get them blocked as well. When Neal had handed him a torch, Kent tossed it onto the thatched roof and laughed when it caught so quickly. When the screams started, Kent danced around the yard and was still standing there when the roof collapsed on the long dead occupants. An hour before sunrise found him back at Neal's house, being given a bath by the most beautiful woman he'd ever met.

"You can fuck her if you want. She likes it hard." Neal sat near him as the sponge was moved over his body. "If you fuck her, I want to join you. I don't want to fuck you physically, mind you, but I want to help you fuck her. She's prime, and I would like to see her perform with another man."

True to his word, Neal never touched him. The woman, however, touched them both in so many ways he still got hard thinking about her. Reaching down to grip his cock, Kent forgot for a moment where he was and found his dick soft and not at all responsive to what he wanted. Having no food would do that to him, he remembered, and he cursed the man who had done this to him again.

"I'll find you. And when I do, I'm going to fuck you up so badly that you'll pray for death." Kent tried to ease his mind, knowing that he would kill the bastard who had done this to him, then he'd find Jade and show her what she'd been missing from him. Tomorrow night he'd go to the shop, kill the mother fucker that left him notes all over the place, and hunt down Jade once and for all.

~~~

Quentin woke and reached for Jade. He came up empty-handed, as she was no longer in the bed. But her pillow was warm so he thought her in the shower. There, too, he was disappointed and reached for her through their link.

"I'm getting Angie ready for school. They have a field trip today and she has to have a permission slip. I'm trying to figure out if I can sign it or if you have to." She sounded so upset that he wanted to go to her but stayed where he was. Going down there now would get his ass kicked, and he didn't want his daughter to see it. There were times when having a very independent woman in your life could be scary.

"I've made arrangements with the school. You're her guardian as much as I am and have permission to do whatever it takes for her

to go to school. I'm sorry. I should have told you yesterday." He smiled. *"You distracted me again."*

"I did no such thing. You came to the Touch and kidnapped me when I was working. How do you expect me to get you ready for the fall festival next week if you're forever coming in and making me all messed up?"

"I love you all messed up." He turned on the shower and stepped into the hot spray as he tried to get her to come up and let him muss her again. *"Why don't you come up here after Angie is gone and wash my back? I'll make it worth your while."*

"I can't this morning. I have three trucks coming in at eight and nine, and I still have to finish what you took me from yesterday." He grinned as he thought of what he'd done to her when he'd kidnapped her from work. Christ, he simply could not get enough of her body and her. *"Are you even listening to me?"*

He hadn't been but didn't think it was smart of him to say so. *"Yes, you said you were going into work. I got water in my ears and didn't hear the rest."*

"You don't need your ears to listen to me this way. I said Angie needs twenty dollars. I've had to borrow it from Mrs. Douglas, so make sure you pay her back." Quentin had meant to make sure that Jade had her credit cards, but every time he was with her, he forgot everything but being inside of her. Before he could tell her he wanted to see her, she continued talking.

"Blair wants to talk to you about the project you and he are working on. And Sapphire brought over some proofs for you. She said that you need to make a decision on the color today so she can get them printed. I like the blue ones, if it matters."

"It does and just tell her that we want them in blue. Also, this thing with Blair, it's about the newspaper ad that's coming out for the festival. Can you meet with him and see what it's about? I have to go to the bank and set up the accounts for the businesses. I won't be but a few hours, and I know that you wanted to get this in the

paper tomorrow." Quentin was putting his tie together when he entered the kitchen, but all he found there was Mrs. Douglas. "I missed them again, didn't I?"

"You did. But the little one left you a note, and your missus said she'd call you later. Also there are several calls for you already this morning. Mr. Blair said for you to call him first thing. He said that it's important." Quentin nodded at her as he read over the phone messages. "You should know that the missus is planning dinner for tonight. She hopes you'll be here."

Quentin took the offered cup of coffee and sat down. He was smiling over Angie's note to him as the phone rang. He heard Mrs. Douglas telling the caller that he was there and to wait. She told him it was Mr. Blair.

"You're a hard man to reach," Blair said in way of greeting. "I've already set up a time to meet with Jade on the article we're running, but I need a quote from you. There is some talk about how you bought the place for your soon-to-be wife and you're just letting her play."

Quentin smiled. "And it's for the most part true. Do you suppose we should let them run with it or tell them the truth?"

"Nah, let them run with it. When it starts to die down, I'll give them something else. Advertising is free for us, and we get your name out in the papers at the same time. But I do need to talk to you. It's about the school. Did you really set up a surveillance crew there?"

"I did. Is there a problem?" Blair assured him that he'd just been surprised. "Angie goes there, as well as Emerald. And someday your own child will go there along with mine and Thad's. I figured that it was the least I could do for my new family."

"I hate to point out that you are spending a great deal of money in my pack. You should get permission for that sort of thing." There was humor there, and Quentin knew that Blair wasn't upset. "What if I wanted to do it?"

"I'll split the cost of the crew that monitors the cameras. What's this really about? Has something happened?" There was a long silence, and Quentin got nervous. "Blair, what's going on?"

"I'm terrified, if you want the truth. I'm going to be a father soon, and my child is going to have to be out there. With humans and other creatures that I suddenly don't trust but always did before. What the fuck is wrong with me?" Quentin laughed. "It's not fucking funny, you asshole. I'm scared someone will hurt what's mine."

"I know the feeling." Quentin decided that he could help the big man out on this one. "When Angie's mother was killed just after our daughter was born, I wouldn't leave the house for anything. I did all my work from home, had groceries delivered. Hell, I even had someone else start my car for me daily just to make sure if I did need it, it wouldn't blow up on me. Then I had to take her to her doctor's appointment."

"She got hurt despite what you did to protect her? I tell you, that's what I mean. I'm putting her in a padded room and leaving her there until she's in her thirties. More if I have to. Christ, what will I do when she starts to date?" Quentin heard Blair breathing hard as he continued. "Quentin, I can't do this."

"Of course you can. And she wasn't sick. It was her appointment set up by her mom. Anyway, I couldn't convince the doctor to come to my house. Then I got to thinking I didn't want him in my house. By the time I made it to the appointment, I was a mess. And Angie knew it. She was screaming her head off, and nothing I could do would help her. But the nurse knew what to do. Scooped her right up out of my arms and patted her bottom and rocked her." Quentin smiled at the memory. "She didn't hurt her or try to take her from me. She simply soothed her, something I couldn't do because I was freaking out. You can't protect them from everything. And you shouldn't. Angie is a brave, smart little girl because she's been in the world. You'll just have to tell them the truth when you can and hope to Christ when the time comes, they'll know what to do."

"Like she did at the school." Quentin told him yes. "And what if someone—?"

"Blair, my man, there is always going to be a 'what if.' No matter what you do to try to keep them in a perfect world, you're so not going to be able to do it. The world? It's just not perfect."

They talked for a few more minutes. Then they ended the call. Quentin was going out the door when the phone rang again. This time he answered it. He felt his skin tighten on his body when the voice at the other end spoke.

"I have your daughter. I have a whole school of little kiddies. Did you know that their blood is the finest of wines to us? Oh, and your fucking guard is dead. Did you really think that he'd stop me?" Quentin reached for Blair as soon as the man spoke again. "The kiddies are all going to die if you don't bring me that fucking cunt Jade. I want her. Now, you mother fucker."

"Who is this and how do I know you have my daughter?" His heart stopped beating for several seconds when he heard her scream for him. "Tell me where you are, because when I get there, I'm going to fucking kill you."

The laughter only pissed him off more. Quentin told Blair word for word what the vampire was saying. Blair told him he was on his way to his house.

"I'm at the little school. Whoever you hired to ward this place should have known that a public place isn't going to keep me out. And now...." Another scream...this one sounded painful rather than terrified. "And now, I have so many playmates that I just don't know where to start. Be here in one hour or so help me I'll kill a child every ten seconds. And I will, too, starting with your pretty little girl."

The phone went dead, but before he put the handset in the cradle, Sloan was standing there in front of him. Quentin told him everything that the vamp said, and then told him what he was going to do once he got him.

"I'm going to make him pay for this. He's killed off my entire family and he's fucking not going to hurt my child." Sloan nodded. "I have to tell Jade. I have to.... I can't tell her on the phone."

Sloan disappeared and returned seconds later with Jade in his arms. She had been in the process of pulling off her coat apparently, and stumbled when he released her. Jade turned on Sloan so quickly that she'd hit him twice before anyone could stop her.

"Jade, Kent has Angie." She froze and turned to him slowly. "He just called me. Sloan brought you here so that I could tell you in person. I didn't...I couldn't...oh Christ, honey, he hurt her. She screamed and I know he hurt her."

He pulled her into his arms and held her as he sobbed. He couldn't lose her. She was his world and he wanted her there. When she pulled back from him, he looked at her as she started barking orders. He was both impressed and terrified. Christ, he loved her.

"Get over to the school and see what they have in the way of security." Blair nodded to her as she caught him as soon as he walked in the door. She turned to Sapphire. "Contact Emerald and find out which room he has them in, and then find us the plans to the school. We can work better if we're not blind."

He had a computer brought to the dining room where they were all assembled and brought up the cameras. Two had been destroyed, and all the others were static but one. The one where the children were being held was working just fine. Angie was sitting with seventeen little kids, and they could see Kent pacing back and forth with a small boy in his arms. He did not look happy.

"Emerald and five teachers are being held in the closet. He's done something to the doors and she can't get them opened. They're here." Sapphire pointed to the screen where there was no picture feed. "She said that other than one of them being bitten, they're all fine. But he's threatened them."

"Threatening them and hurting them are two different things right now." Quentin agreed, but he was no less terrified for the people there, and he was sure Jade was as well. When she turned to him, he stood up from the table and waited. "I have to go in."

"No, you're not. He wants you, and the last thing I'm going to do is put you in a place where he'll have all my family." She shook her head. "I'm serious, Jade. I don't want you going in there."

"I'm not going alone." He looked around the room then back at her as she smiled. "You're going in, too. As a big, bad animal. Your choice, too. I'm sure he'll be surprised as hell about that, and more so since I'm not the cowering fool I once was. I'm not taking his fucking shit again."

"You think we can take him?" Quentin liked the idea that they'd be going together. He had a feeling that he'd not be able to stop her anyway, no matter how much he wanted to. But if he was with her, then he'd stand a fighting chance of keeping her safe.

"Oh, I know we can. Once he gets a good look at what the fuck we are, he'll surrender. And if not?" She shrugged. "Then we end his fucking ass."

Quentin liked this plan very much. So much so that he started barking his own orders. By the time he made a call to the school and talked with Ballard again to set up the exchange, he was as confident as he'd ever been in any meeting in his entire career.

Chapter 15

Angie watched the big man walk back and forth. He was very mad, and she almost smiled at that. He was mad because her daddy had told him that they were coming, but if one of them was hurt, he was going to kill him. The big vampire had told them how stupid her daddy was, and she wanted to stand up and punch him in the nose. But Lilly, the little girl sitting next to her, said to be still and not make him see them.

She knew what she meant. They were all being quiet now that he'd taken Mike. He'd been crying like a little baby, and the man had picked him up and almost shook him to death. He was quiet now, but they could see that he wasn't dead. He looked at them every time he passed them. Angie felt sorry for the boy. He'd peed in his pants, and she'd just die if she did that.

"Which one of you fucking brats is Angie Witt?" She started to stand up when someone behind her pushed her back down. "You heard me. Who is the little bitch?"

"I am." Lilly stood up and grabbed her hand as she stood there. "I'm Angie Witt. And I want my daddy."

Before the man could come at her, which was what Angie was sure he was going to do, a girl behind her stood up, too. "I'm Angie Witt. And I want my daddy."

Three more girls stood up and said the same thing. When Lilly squeezed her hand, Angie stood up and said that she was Angie and she wanted her daddy as well. When all the girls were standing there, he looked at them all and growled. Angie wanted to laugh. She'd been growled at before, and he wasn't very good at it.

"You'll stop lying to me and tell me who the real one is. I'm not fucking around here. Who is the Witt girl?" He waited, tapping his foot as if he expected them to do what he wanted. "I'll start killing you all off if I don't get the answer I want."

"We gave it to you." She looked at the others, then back at him as she continued. "You can't just ask for something and then when you get the answer, just want us to do something else. It's not fair. Why don't you go away?"

He dropped Mike and came toward her, but she wasn't afraid. She put up her fists like she saw on television and hit him in the nose when he was close. He backed away, but she didn't put her hands down.

"Why, you little bitch!" Everyone in the room stood up then and milled around her. Angie felt like that woman Joan of Arc with her troops behind her. "I should simply kill you all."

"You try, and I'll hit you again." He stared at her for several seconds. Angie wasn't sure what he was thinking, but his eyes turned really red, like the crayon she'd been using before he came in. "I'm not afraid of you. None of us are."

"You're going to pay for that." When he reached for her, she dodged but not nearly quickly enough. His hand touched her face, and she felt the sting of it all the way to her toes. When he tried to get her again, she moved faster. Because, despite what she'd told him, she was now very afraid. But then something happened and the door behind her exploded.

"Get the fuck away from my daughter." Angie wanted to see who Jade was talking about, but a giant wolf came into the room. Then a big bear and a panther. She took a step back but held her ground when the man looked at her again.

"Your daughter? You didn't have any children yet, Jade. Not when I knew you. And this kid couldn't possibly be yours. She had a back bone, something you could only dream of having." The man glanced at her, then back at Jade. "You should only hope to be like her."

"You think so?" Jade laughed, then put her hand out. Angie went to her without thought to the man. "This is my daughter, Angela Witt. And hurting her just signed your death certificate."

The man reached for her again, but Jade was quicker this time and shoved her behind her. Jade stood up to the man in a way that made her look a hundred feet tall, Angie thought, and she knew that she'd love her forever and ever. And when someone picked her up and took her down the hall, she screamed until she realized it was Sloan.

"It's okay, baby. I got you. Your new mother is really something bad-assed, isn't she?" Angie nodded and smiled at him. "That's my girl. Can you show me where the others are? I want to save your aunt and the other teachers."

Angie took him to the room that held the five teachers. There was a body lying on the floor, but Sloan told her not to look. When he finally pulled the door off the wall, she stood back while the others came out. Emerald grabbed her in a big hug and held her as she cried.

"I'm okay, Aunt Emerald. I swear. He only cut me a little bit." Emerald nodded but didn't stop squeezing her. It was okay as far as Angie was concerned. She kind of needed the hug anyway. When they were helped out the door and into the parking lot, Angie was surprised to see so many people.

Annabelle, her new grandma, pulled her to her and held her and Emerald while she sobbed. Angie decided it was pretty wonderful to have a really nice family.

When the guy from the ambulance told her that her mom or dad would have to fix her wound, she didn't correct him. From now on, she had a mommy and a daddy, and she was going to call Jade that as soon as she came out. Sitting as quietly as she could, she thought of the other kids. When Ruby came to her and held her hand, Angie laid her head on her shoulder.

"Will Mom and Dad be okay?" Ruby laughed. "I don't want them to be hurt. I just got a mom, and I want to call her that."

"She'll be fine. They both will. They'll take care that this man doesn't hurt anyone again. Especially not you. They love you very much." She looked at the wound. "Do you know why the medic can't stitch up your wounds?" Angie shook her head. "Because a vampire scratched you. And one of them will have to lick it clean first. The reason one of us can't do it is because we'd have your blood and that would mean that we would be a part of you. Does that make sense?"

"You mean you can find me." Ruby nodded. "My uncle Roger told me that, too, when he licked me. He said that he'd be able to find me no matter what. I was afraid for him to find me, but not you guys. You kind of like me, right?"

"Oh honey, we love you very much." Angie watched the school with the others. But her eyes kept closing, and she was having a hard time staying awake. When Ruby shifted on the bed and laid Angie's head on her lap, Angie finally fell asleep. Her parents would make sure things were all right. She was sure of it.

~~~

Jade watched the other children as they began to sit. None of them were hurt, but she'd bet her last dollar that they were terrified. The little boy that had been lying so still when they entered had been pulled into the tight little group and was now watching them with terror-filled eyes. She wanted to hug them all to her.

"You're going to stay here, and I'll let the others go." Kent crossed his arms over his chest as if she'd do just what he said. "Now, Jade. You know how much I hate to be disobeyed."

Quentin roared at him and took a step forward. His panther was beautiful, but she was afraid that he was no match for the big vamp. When Kent laughed, Blair moved forward, too, but he didn't make a sound. Out of the corner of her eye, Jade saw Sloan appear in the room behind the children. He touched the first child and disappeared with him. It was working.

"I'm not going to do anything at all with you, Kent. I'm so over your ass, it's not even funny anymore. And as of yesterday, all that money you took from me is now back where it belongs. The credit card companies are looking for you, by the way." He snorted at her. "What you did is considered grand larceny. That's a long prison time. And there is no dark place for you to hide once they get you. Of course, you'll never make it to trial, but I thought you should know."

Three more children disappeared. And when Sloan winked at her, she noticed another man with him who was now helping. It was hard on them, she was sure. The sun had been up for nearly five hours by then. But soon there was only two left, and Sloan was holding them both when he nodded at her. Then he was gone.

"You're going to pay for this. You know that, right?" She noticed that he moved away from the windows again, and realized he must be getting to the point that he could no longer stand the sun. "You're going to have to find shelter soon. How are you going to do that with us in your way?"

"Because you'll move or I'll kill the brats. And I know what a softy you are when it comes to children. You got all teary when I nearly killed that fucking brat next door. Remember him? All he did was cry and whine about everything. I should have ended his life even though you said no." She laughed at him, and Jade could see that it startled him. "You think that I won't do it?"

"Do what to whom?" She waved her hand around the room. "You're going to kill the brats? How do you plan to do that?"

"By breaking each of their skinny little necks while you watch." He took another step from the window before he continued. "Then I'm going to rip your fucking throat out while I fuck you."

Quentin snarled at him, but Kent only laughed. She knew that the moment he turned and realized he no longer had a bargaining chip, he was going to attack. Jade only hoped that when he did, they were all ready. She didn't want anyone hurt. Not unless it was Kent.

"Come with me now, Jade, and I'll let all these people live. I have no qualms with any of them. It's you I want, and I will have you. It's only a matter of time, and we both know it. Bringing your big bad alpha here. These other animals are all for show, but they will die unless you cooperate with me." He put out his hand as if she'd simply take it. "Come on. It's the way things need to be."

"No." He laughed slightly at her refusal. "Never again will you treat me or anyone else like you did me. You're a monster, plain and simple."

"So their deaths will be on your head." He turned then and stood looking at the empty space behind him for several seconds before he looked over his shoulder at her. The smile he had on his face was friendly. His fangs showed, long and dark with stain, and she saw him morph into something that…something that she had no idea of until he was finished.

He really and truly was a monster. And what he'd shifted to was bigger than she'd imagined him to be able to be. Claws, long and sharp, grew from his fingers until they were nearly twice the length of his arm. His feet burst from his shoes to look the same as his hands. Dark nails erupted from the ends of his toes that were stained with dried blood and filth. She took a step back when his back seemed to move until there were wings, wide and black, spread wide in the small room. When he turned, his face, too, had morphed into something that no longer looked like a man, but a collection of all animals each fighting for space. Eyes stared back at her, yellowed with evil. Jade was suddenly terrified beyond anything she'd ever encountered.

"You will do as I say." Kent's voice thundered across the room to her, blowing her hair from her face. The heat and the putrid smell of his breath nearly took her breath away. "You'll do it now."

"No." Her voice was strong, and she lifted her chin. "You aren't anything to me. I will not obey you ever again."

When he lunged at her, she moved. Her plan was to shift and attack, but she was tossed aside, and her back hit the wall behind her. She thought it was Kent who'd hit her, but when she tried to sit up, she saw that Quentin had done it. And now he was tearing at Kent's throat. Before she could move to pull him away, Sloan had her around the waist and was holding her back.

"He has to do this. If not for you, then for his family." She looked Sloan in the eyes. "You know that I would never let him be hurt, but he will win at this. I swear to you, Quentin will kill this beast."

Quentin was tossed away, and Kent roared. As soon as Quentin was on his feet, he lunged at the beast as he shifted from panther to wolf. His wounds were gone, the bleeding stopped. And he attacked more viciously, tearing at the beast's throat as his clawed feet tore at his soft belly. Each time he was thrown away, Quentin came back stronger, shifting between the two of his own beasts to keep him healed and strong.

Kent had no such help. His throat was bloodied, and his open wounds sprayed blood all over the room. His left arm hung lank, and his right was almost as useless. He was also burning from the sun, as Quentin kept knocking him back into it faster than he could heal. And he was growing weaker. Every time he tried to throw Quentin off, it was with less power, less of a punch. Quentin was winning, but it wasn't over yet.

Kent seemed to know he was beaten. He began making more attempts at killing Quentin rather than stopping him from hurting him. He was grabbing things up, pencils and other items within his reach, to stab into Quentin. For the most part, he dodged them, but some he could not. Soon it was obvious that both men were at their end, but still Sloan held her. When Quentin dropped back and shook his head, his body heaved with exhaustion and loss of blood. When Kent tried to attack again, Jade had had enough and shoved Sloan away and shifted in mid-leap, going straight for the beast's throat.

Silver tainted his blood. Kent had not a great deal in his system but enough to make her hurt. When she ripped at his throat, she felt him stab at her belly but didn't let go. She was going to end this even if it killed her.

"Get away from him, Jade. He'll hurt you. Let me do this." She felt Quentin's pain when he touched her mind. Knew that if he tried again, even if it was only to push Kent back, he'd die.

Working harder than she ever had before, she tore deeper into Kent and thought about all the things he'd done to her, made her do and say. She remembered each time he hit her, bit into her throat in the name of love. When she got the first statement where he'd charged over eight thousand dollars in her name on a cruise that he didn't even go on. Then she remembered the scratches on Angie's face. The way her skin was open and bleeding. Jade lifted her head and looked him right in the eye and then, using her nails, dug his heart out.

He dropped her then and stared at her for several seconds before he went to his knees. She crushed the heart under her paw while she kept her eyes on him. He continued to stare at her while blood pooled between them.

"Why?" He looked at his destroyed heart, then at her as life faded from his eyes. "Why would you do that to me?"

She never got to answer him because he suddenly disappeared. He didn't leave the room or even use magic, but disintegrated right there. His ash mingled with his blood, and soon it, too, was gone.

As soon as Quentin touched her with his head, she moved her body along his and marked him. He growled low but didn't say anything. Her legs began to feel wobbly, and her head started to spin when she was suddenly looking into the face of Sloan.

"Let it come to you, Jade. It won't hurt as badly if you do." She tried to pull away from him, but he held her firmly.

"I'm sorry, love; I had hoped that Quentin would get this and not you, but this might be better anyway. Let it roll over you."

Her mind started to feel woozy, and she felt her knees buckle. Quentin was saying something to her, but she couldn't make it out. There was screaming in her head, and she tried to make it stop, but she was fading now, faster. And she went down.

"I'm sorry, Jade, I truly am, but I wasn't allowed to tell anyone. It was…it's not something we share as vampires." He still held her so that she could only see his face. "It's almost here now. Then you're going to hurt like hell. I'm so sorry. So very—"

She pitched forward and felt her body seem to leave itself. When she opened her eyes again, Sloan was being attacked by Blair, but she simply couldn't move. Before everything faded out, she saw Quentin drop, too, and blood pour from his nose. Christ, they were both dying.

Chapter 16

Blair was seated in the back of the court room and held onto Angie's hand while the lawyer that was stating his case seemed to drone on and on. When the little girl squeezed his hand, he looked down at her. Then he leaned down to hear her speak.

"Does that man ever shut up? He's been talking and talking forever." She made the word "forever" sound like it had a great deal more syllables than it actually had. "Why don't he just say that they were wrong and we can go get ice cream?"

"Doesn't, not don't, and that's not the way it works. They have to present their evidence. Then there has to be a trial. Once that is over, there will more than likely be appeals, and that could last until your children's children are born." She rolled her eyes at him, and he felt stupid. Blair noted that she did that a lot...made a grown-up feel like he or she was the dumbest person on earth. And he doubted very much if she even knew she was doing it. "What do you say you and I go and get some lunch at the diner across the street when they take a break? They have pie."

"I don't like apple pie." He nodded, trying hard not to laugh. She'd made that sound like it was something that had crawled out from under a rock. "And I want pie before lunch. I've been very good today while you watched me, haven't I?"

"You have." Blair looked up when the judge started speaking. He was actually reading out loud, so Blair tuned him out. He looked at Jade and Quentin as they sat there as if they had not a care in the world. Which, he supposed, they didn't. Who would be able to guess that they were not just wolves sitting there, but two of the richest people in the world? And thanks in great part to the magic that Jade got when she killed Kent, they were now the strongest beings as well.

He'd nearly killed Sloan when Jade had dropped to the floor. Then when Quentin had done the same, blood pouring from their noses and ears, he'd pulled out a long dagger and was ready to shove it into Sloan's chest when a being appeared in the room and held his arm.

"I would not if I were you." He took the blade from his limp hand, and it disappeared in his robes. "You will allow this to happen, or they both will die."

"They're dying now." The being shook his head. "Look at them. They're bleeding to death. He's let them be killed."

"I do not need to look. I can feel them." He knelt down to his face, and Blair had had a feeling he was being sized up for something. "You are a good man. They will need rest. Give them peace as well. When they are rested, I will return. Not before then."

Then he'd disappeared. That had been weeks ago. This trial had been set up almost immediately, and now Jade was being sued by the credit card companies as well as named in Kent Ballard's death. Blair was still trying to figure out how anyone had found out Ballard was dead. The man had been living a fake life for hundreds of years, and now they cared?

"So you're telling me that this man, this…what was his name again?" The judge looked at the papers, then at the bailiff. He told him. "Kent Ballard had the permission of this young lady here to apply for credit cards, then run them up to hell and back, ruining her credit. Is that what you're trying to convey to me?"

"She did allow him to do so, sir. She had broken it off with him and more than likely felt badly for leaving." The judge snorted. "How else would he have gotten the information to do this if not from her?"

"Same way that bastard did that stole my identity and charged a dildo to my Amazon account. They're always looking for a scam. Could be he just took what he wanted." The judge glared at the room when they snickered. "Nothing funny about identity theft. They'll rob you blind in a heartbeat."

"Your Honor, this is a simple case of a woman trying to latch onto an estate that is worth billions to get herself out of trouble." The lawyer looked at the table where Jade was sitting, and she blew him a kiss. "Your Honor, could you please have Miss Erickson conduct herself in a proper manner?"

"It's Witt, you moron. I've told you that eight times now. Get it right or else." Jade stood up and was pulled back down by her lawyer. But the man was laughing while he did it. Quentin was laughing as well. Angie put herself in Blair's lap, and he held her. This might turn out to be better than he thought.

"She has told you a great many times. And as far as her wanting his money, do you have any idea who her husband is?" The judge asked the lawyer, then shook his head when he said he did not. "You read anything besides the comics when you read the paper? That man sitting there is the richest man in the world. Not almost the richest, but the main dog. He has no more use for this idiot's money than…well, he's got no use for it."

"But Your Honor? She owes over fifty thousand dollars to one of our cards alone. And twice that on two more." The judge just shook his head. "You can't mean to let this go?"

"Why the hell would someone give a girl that big a line of credit in the first place? When this card was taken out, she had less than five thousand in the bank, two part-time jobs, and a car as old as I am." The judge picked up several sheets of paper as he continued. "It says here that after not making the minimum payment for three months, you increased her limit to double the original amount. Why?"

"She had a good credit score. And she asked." The judge tossed the papers on his desk and leaned back in his chair. "There are standards that we have to maintain here, sir. If we are required to write off this much debt, then others will try the same thing."

"Then perhaps it might be beneficial to you to do a better background check. Call the person who is supposed to be applying for that much credit, and be a great deal smarter when it comes to doling out that much money." He sat up and looked around the sparsely filled court room. "Case dismissed. All charges against Mrs. Witt are dropped." The lawyer stood up again, and the judge only glared.

"And the murder of Mr. Ballard, sir? What do you wish to do about that? The prosecution hasn't produced a body, no one has seen my wife around him since she left over a year ago, and other than this man telling her he was dead, we've no other reason to believe he's not out somewhere bilking another woman just like he did Jade." Quentin looked at the other lawyer before continuing his plea to the judge. "We've been married for four days, sir. And in those four days we've been stuck here going over material that, frankly, is a lie."

"I agree." The judge looked at the lawyer that was seated just in front of Blair and Angie and told him to stand. "You got a body? Witnesses to the fact that she killed this man? Even a drop of his blood on her clothing, prints? Anything at all?"

The man said no. "But we do have reason to believe she was involved in his—"

"Reason to believe? Do you know that there are fourteen other women out there that he's done the same thing to? And untold many more that could tell you the same thing? And probably want the man dead, too? Are you going to charge all of them on your *reason*?"

The man didn't say anything but sat down. Things were going just as Quentin had said they would. There was nothing to hold her on, and less on the credit card charges. When the judges gavel came down hard and he stood up, so did the others in the room. Before he and Angie could make their way to the couple, they were already kissing.

"You guys do that all the time. I'm so embarrassed." Angie looked up at him with the most bored look he'd ever seen. "Do you and Aunt Sapphire kiss all the time? It's so gross. I wish they'd just shake hands or something."

Blair picked her up. "But then you'd never get a brother or sister. You'd like some wouldn't you? Someone to boss around and teach all sorts of tricks to keep you out of trouble?"

"Don't help her, Blair. She's in enough trouble already." Blair looked at Quentin, then back at Angie, who was a bright shade of red. "She decided that we needed a cat. The poor thing came into the house and nearly tore the cook up trying to get away from the scent in the house. I swear it will be a month before we get a decent meal out of her."

"You didn't." Angie nodded at him. "You know that your family is all canines, right? And that when a feline comes into the picture, they want to run. Someone could have gotten seriously hurt."

"But I want a pet. And mommy said that I had to find something without fur. The kitty didn't have any fur." Blair had a feeling that little Miss Angie was going to be a handful, and he hoped to Christ that she didn't teach his children any of this. But then again, it would be fun. Blair handed her to her dad as he walked away. He had to go and find his own wife, as they were going to go find them a nursery.

~~~

"You won today." Quentin moved up behind his new wife as she stood at the sink, and kissed her neck. "You said that you'd lose and if you didn't, you'd do whatever I wanted."

Her scent perfumed the air and he licked her neck before nipping at it. She moaned and gripped the counter harder. Quentin felt his cock swell. Christ, he loved this woman.

"You meant that I'd let you remodel the office to suit yourself. I didn't think you had to bargain me with sex." She turned in his arms and put hers around his shoulders. "Do you think that I'd not do anything you wanted?"

Quentin rocked into her and was rewarded with a deep moan. "We've not played since the stupid trial started. I want to take you out back and run you down again. You've no idea how many times I've thought of slamming my cock into you from behind."

There were times since the day she'd killed Ballard that he was worried for her. She would stare off into space, and he'd have to touch her to bring her back to him. He, too, was having weird out of mind experiences, and had finally gone to Sloan about them. His news wasn't very comforting.

"It's the magic that you inherited from Ballard. Some of it's tainted and will...well, it's tempting you to follow him. In his footsteps." Quentin had started to shake his head, but Sloan continued. "It'll fade after a while. You'll get used to not seeing what he's done, planned, or even attempted. I swear to you you're going to be fine."

Quentin had told Jade what it was, but she, like him, didn't want to believe it. There was something so...black about the man that had them both waking in the night with sweat all over their bodies.

"Angie goes to school in ten minutes. In eleven minutes I'll meet you in the yard. I need to run, too." He let her go, knowing that once he got her outside and playing in the snow, as they'd done yesterday, she'd be all right. "Oh, and if you think you're going to be the one taking me, big boy, think again. I've got plans for you."

He thought his cock was going to explode. Moving carefully out of the bathroom, he went to get dressed in the soft terry pants that he'd been told to get. They were tear-aways, pants that had Velcro down both legs so that in the event that he shifted, maybe he'd be able to put them back on. So far, that hadn't been an issue. But today, he was looking forward to testing the theory.

As soon as she came out onto the deck with him, he could smell her. Quentin could feel her coming down a hall toward him and smell her when she was aroused. All these new abilities were a little overwhelming, but not as bad as they'd been at first. Now he could tone down the noise, but the scents were something that still caught him by surprise.

"You can smell me." He nodded at her as she wrapped her arms around him from behind. "I can smell you, too. Did you know that we can find each other no matter where we are?"

"Yes. I've finally read that book Blair gave me. Do you suppose that anything that Ballard gave us will change anything for us now?" He knew of a few things but hadn't told her yet. The one that frightened him most was the fact that they now had the ability to live forever. "Other than the things we've figured out."

"You mean like the fact that we can shift into other animals? That one scared the crap out of me." He laughed and turned in her arms and kissed her nose as she continued. "I don't want to think about Ballard now. I want to run with you. I want to chase you in, then run you to ground."

They stepped back from each other and shifted at the same time. The feeling of being something entirely different wasn't just amazing to him. It was still, even after doing it so much lately, unbelievable. The fact that he could be a human at one moment then any animal he wanted had blown him away.

Jade took off first. Her leap over the railing took his breath away, and she was nearly to the tree line when he realized he should be going after her. Leaping over the railing himself, he was suddenly glad that she wasn't there to see his fumble. His foot had caught in the top and he'd nearly fallen on his face.

Quentin caught her scent the moment he entered the woods. He found her sitting quietly staring off into space again. Thinking she was having another thought like Ballard's, he nearly tackled her to bring her back, but he spied the group of deer just ahead of them. There was a single buck, four females, and seven fawn. It was late in the year for them to be so young, and he decided that he'd set out hay and straw for them for the coming months. When he settled beside her, she looked at him.

"I want a child with you. Now; I want a child with you now. I love Angie very much and would love to give her siblings. I don't know what I'd do without mine." He moved his head along her fur as she turned back to the deer. *"We're going to live for a very long time, Quentin. I want to have many, many children with you."*

"I do as well. We'll give Angie as many as she wants and then some." He laughed when he thought of the conversation that was going to be. His daughter was very smart and would more than likely tell them a thing or two about being new parents again.

For some reason they seemed to be of the same mind after the deer moved on. Without words to each other, they shifted to human and he touched her body gently with his fingers. Closing his eyes, he moved his fingers over all of her, starting with her face.

Warm flesh with a touch of dew from the snow mingled together. They were warmer than if they'd been human, and he was glad to have her like this in nature. Touching her shoulders, he moved down along her arms, then to her hands. When she curled her fingers into his, he opened his eyes and kissed her on the mouth.

"I want you." She nodded. "Lay down so that I may make love to you. I want to fill you with my seed."

"I'm in heat." He nodded, knowing that today they would create a child. "I'm afraid. I don't...what if he's like me?"

"That would be the most wonderful gift you could give me." He helped her to the ground and settled between her thighs. His cock ached to be deep inside of her, but he was in no hurry. Moving slowly down with his mouth, he took her nipple into his mouth, then suckled at her entire breast. "When you come, I'm going to bite you. And when I do, I want you to scream."

"Yes," she hissed at him. Entering her slowly had sweat bead on his back and trickle slowly down his spine. He wanted to pound into her, but also wanted to take her as gently as he could. When she locked her ankles around his hips, he buried himself as deeply as he could go.

"Christ, do you have any idea what it feels like to know that you're mine forever?" She nodded and arched up to take him deeper. "Jade, Christ, honey, I'm never going to get to go slowly if you keep this up."

"Take me, Quentin. Fill me up and make me come." Her body rippled around his as she dug her nails deep into his back. He knew when she drew blood and felt his body quicken with it. "I'm coming."

Her scream tore through the forest and bounced off trees until it echoed back to them. Moving faster now, in and out of her, he felt his own release coming on him hard. When she licked the crease where his shoulder met his neck, he did the same to her. When he sank his canines deep into her flesh, she did the same to him, triggering the most powerful climax he'd ever had.

Stars danced behind his lids as he tried his best to hold on. Darkness seemed to play with him as he pounded deeper into her. When she cried out again, shouting out his name like a litany, he tore at her flesh and marked her again. When he came again, he knew that he was spent. Pulling her tightly against him as he dropped onto her, he rolled to his back, bringing her to cover him. The cold snow had him laughing.

"We're going to have to bring out blankets if you're going to seduce me like this often." Her soft moan had him realize that she'd been as affected by their loving making as he'd been. Her smile made him grin, the sated look in her face had him wanting to crow like a fool. Closing his eyes for a moment, he had such a vivid image of her swollen with child that he had to reach down to make sure it wasn't true.

They stood up and dressed. Quentin found that he couldn't stop touching her, and was glad that she wanted the same. According to the book he'd read, wolves were a pack for a reason. They needed to be together, and touching was a big part of it. When they made their way into the house, the phone was ringing. Mrs. Douglas answered it on the second ring.

"It's Mr. Sloan, sire. He's a might upset about something. I thought to have you call him back, as he's called three times today, but he will not listen to me." She tisked at the phone as he took it from her. "Men think the world will end if they've no one to talk to someone about their problems. Worse than women, I think."

All he got to say was hello before Sloan started talking. "Did you know this? Did you have any fucking idea what they did to me? I'm not going to put up with this crap. I'm seven thousand years old, set in my ways. I will not take a mate just because they deem it so."

"Slow down and tell me what you're talking about. Who will make you take a mate? And what the hell does your age have to do with it?" Quentin had a moment of panic when he realized his friend was seven thousand years old and he could conceivable live to be that old, but Sloan was talking again.

"They sent me to watch her. I can't send Rufus either; it has to be me. I was told it was my reward for my service in helping with you and your mate. What the fuck is that supposed to mean, helping you? All I did was grab up a bunch of kids. And now I have a mate? No fucking way. I want you to talk to them in my behalf. You owe me." Quentin started laughing and the more Sloan bitched, the harder he laughed. Before he could gain any control over his mirth, the man was standing in his kitchen glaring at him.

"I do not find this to be the least bit funny." Quentin laughed harder until tears streamed down his face and dripped off his chin. "I shall simply refuse to help them from now on. That will settle this."

Quentin finally got some control over himself as Jade sat on his lap. She stared at Sloan for several minutes until the man squirmed.

"Who's your mate, and what do you have against having one? And you'd better have a better reason than the one that put Quentin into hysterics." Sloan huffed at Jade, and she cocked a brow at him. "Well?"

"I don't want a mate, because I'm fine without one. It's all fine and good for some people, but not for me. Especially her." Sloan flushed. "Not that I even know her, but that's no reason I should be forced to take a mate."

"Who is she?" Jade asked him again. This time he sat before saying anything. When he laid his head on the table and seemed to be thinking, Quentin got worried. And when Sloan mumbled something, he had to have him repeat it.

"I said your sister, Opal." He glared at him, then at Jade. "Your sister Opal is my mate, and I do not want her."

Chapter 17

Opal was enjoying Paris. She'd never traveled before outside of the United States, and was having so much fun she decided she might extend her vacation for another month. Who did she have back home to need her? Besides, she'd done really well at the show last month, and she was determined to have a good time before she had to go back and start making things again for the next one. Or, she thought, she'd open her own store. People really seemed to like what she did.

"Excusez-moi, mademoiselle? Savez-vous où je pourrais trouver l'Hôtel Marcus?" It took her a few minutes to try to translate what the man was asking her. But she beamed when she knew it.

"The Hotel Marcus is on Seventh near the Tea and Crumbles." She hoped that's what she told him anyway when she repeated it in French. When he nodded and stepped around her, she let him go without another thought. People were so nice here.

When she was bumped hard from behind, she turned to say she was sorry. She'd been looking at her map again and sometimes would forget there were others moving around her. But the man said something else to her, and she had a feeling it wasn't nice. When she looked around, she realized that they were alone. Where had all the other people gone?

"You'll come with me, my dear." Opal backed up and blindly put her map in her bag. "Running will do you no good. I've your scent now, and I plan to take you somewhere we can…talk."

"No. I don't know who you are, but I'm not going anywhere with you." She saw a second man coming out of the alley, and he didn't look all that happy to see her either. "I'll scream."

"And who do you suppose would hear you? I've protected you from the tourists around here. It's just you and me. And I do not like to be told no." The man was coming faster now, but he seemed to be so far away. Opal had a thought that the man in front of her had no idea about the one behind him, and decided that she didn't want to go with either of them. Turning on her heel, she took off running until she hit a wall. No, not a wall, but another man.

Looking up into the face of the man that held her to him, she felt a little faint. Men like this one just didn't touch women like her. She tried to struggle away from him, but he snapped at her to be still.

"Sloan? What are you doing here? I thought you were firmly entrenched in the States." They didn't seem to be friends, and the man from the alley confirmed it when he grabbed the first one around the throat with his massive arms.

"I think you know why I'm here. And you'll leave her alone. She's not yours." The man looked confused as Sloan continued. "You touch any of the women from this pack and I'll personally tear your heart out."

"As far as I know, this little morsel isn't claimed. And her virginal blood will make me feel like a man who had dined on the finest of meals and drank of the most delicious liquors. You would deny me that?" Sloan pushed her behind him, and she started to run again. But he grabbed her arm just as the man continued. "I will have her, Sloan. You've no right to keep me from her. A meal is a meal, as you well know."

"You'll leave her alone, as I have said, and she is mine." The man looked shocked, and Opal didn't blame him. She no more belonged to him than she did to either of them. Before she could tell either of them she was her own person, Sloan pulled her in front of him so that she faced her attacker.

The air around them seemed to grow thick. Opal opened her mouth to say something when she felt her hair being let down. Sloan moved his hand through her tumble of curls, and she felt her body light on fire. Nothing had ever made her feel this way before, and his touch was heating her up more.

When a moan spilled from her lips, she put her hand over Sloan's to stop his movement to her breast. But he cupped her hand into his and moved it with his to cup her. Her nipples hardened in her bra, and she moaned again.

"I'm going to taste you." She nodded, not caring what he did so long as he didn't stop what he was doing now. "Come for me, Opal, while I taste you."

Her hair was suddenly moved from her shoulder, and Sloan tilted her head. Opal felt his cock harden against her. And when he rocked into her, she grabbed his arm. Christ, she was going to have a climax if he kept this up. Before she could protest, she felt his tongue touch her pounding pulse, and she tried to tighten her legs together to get some relief there. When she felt the sharp pain of his bite, Opal cried out. Not from pain but from the release that rocked through her entire body.

"*Again*," he told her in her mind. "Come for me again so that I can taste it." She had no choice in the matter, and her body reacted violently to his command. She was still trembling with sated relief when he licked her again, sealing the wound he'd inflicted.

"There, she's marked. You'll leave her alone from now on." Opal found herself suddenly standing alone and Sloan near the man. It took her fuddled mind a few seconds to realize what he'd done to her.

He'd marked her. Marked her so that the other man wouldn't touch her. Staggering back a little, she heard someone say her name, but she was humiliated enough. She turned this time and took off running. Christ, what had just happened?

Sitting in her hotel room twenty minutes later, Opal tried her best to tell herself that it was all a dream. She'd been hot and thirsty. Not drinking enough could make a person see and think things like that, she told herself. When she finally stood up and went to the bathroom, Opal stripped off all her clothes and stepped into the hot spray of the shower. Washing her entire body three times did not make her feel any less like it was anything but the truth. She'd been bitten and marked.

Getting out of the shower, she dried herself. Opal was nearly through with her first list of things to pack up when she realized that she was leaving Paris today. The appeal of the place was no longer there, and she knew that she had to go home. When she stepped into the living room, she wasn't overly surprised to see Sloan and the man from the alley sitting in her living room. Ignoring them, she picked up her things and took them back to the bedroom. There was no way she was going to acknowledge either of them. When the door clicked shut behind her, she stiffened but didn't stop packing.

~~~

Sloan watched her fold her shirts and pants and put them into the suitcase. He wasn't sure what he was supposed to say to her, because every line of her body told him she was mad and ready to tangle with him. And while she did, he had a feeling she was going to have nothing on her sisters when it came to having a temper. He cleared his throat, trying his best to soothe her, but she seemed to be very focused on what she was doing instead of him.

"I had to do something. He was going to take you. And my biting you saved you from being his whore." She said something, but he was sure he didn't hear it correctly. "What did you just say?"

"I said, so now I'm yours. Your whore." Sloan felt his temper rise, but he calmed himself with the knowledge that she had no idea what he was to her. "I'm thinking I'd very much like for you to go away. I'm going…I've got a great deal to do today, and I want to be alone."

"I have to talk to you." She turned then, and he had only a second to realize he'd been wrong. She wasn't just mad. She was spitting pissed off, and her wolf was coming. But it was her beauty that took his breath away. Before he could say anything, she had him pinned to the wall and several feet off the floor.

"You'll leave me alone or I'll tear your throat out and spit in your face." He wanted to point out that she was very bad at verbal threats, but she was just fine in the scary department. But he had a feeling, verbal or not, she'd kill him if he didn't do something quickly.

"*I'm your mate.*" Her body seemed to freeze as he spoke through their link. "*I don't want to be, but you're mine until I can figure out a way to stop it.*"

"You marked me." He nodded without much movement. She had him held that tightly. Then she tossed him across the room, and he landed on a chair, shattering it to splitters. He had a moment of worry that all the tales of being unable to harm one's mate were untrue. But she was suddenly across the room, too, when Rufus knocked her away.

He was on the man in a heartbeat, and if Opal hadn't have cried out, he might have killed him. When he turned to her, she had a piece of glass in her chest that she'd gotten when she hit the glass that had been sitting on the table. Christ, there was so much blood...he was at her side immediately.

"Get back." Sloan ignored her and picked her up. She weighed nothing. He wondered if he could convince her to put on some weight before he bit her again. Shutting down that thought because there wasn't going to be any more biting, she cried out again when he tried to look at her wound. Pulling out the glass only made her bleed more, and he knew in that moment that there was no way they were walking away from this unscathed.

"You need to take my blood." The look on her face might have been funny if the situation wasn't so serious. She was losing blood much too fast. He realized she'd cut into an artery. "Opal, you're going to bleed to death if you don't drink from me."

"Fuck off." When she tried to sit up again, he had Rufus hold her. Sloan was actually afraid she'd shift. If she did with the amount of blood she'd lost, it might be her certain death. Tearing into his own wrist, he pressed it to her mouth and commanded her to drink. It wasn't until she was unconscious that he was able to get her to take it. Christ, she was going to die if he didn't do something quickly.

"You're going to convert her if you give her much more." Rufus knew as well as he did that she was dying. "Might save her, but she's going to kill you if you do this."

He had no choice. Sloan either had to convert her to a vampire or she'd die. Neither was an option that he was thrilled with, but letting her die was out of the question. Her family would most assuredly kill him if he did.

"Christ, she's going to hate me for this." He leaned to her throat and bit her hard. Drinking from her as she took his blood was the only way now. When he felt her body begin to take his blood and use it to change her, he sealed the wound at her throat and pulled his wrist from her mouth.

"She's gonna make it, I'm thinking. Might be hard on her with her being so young and all, but I'm thinking you'll pave the way for her. Too bad you lied to her about the mate thing." Sloan stared at his friend until he realized the truth. "Mother fuck, she's your mate? You just fucking converted your mate not an hour after you met her? She is going to kill you."

Sloan ordered Rufus out of the room. His laughter was putting him on edge, and he was terrified enough as it was about this. Looking down at the lovely woman on the bed, he wondered how he was going to tell Blair and the rest when he felt the man touch his mind.

"You fucking bastard." Sloan nodded his agreement at the man. *"I'm going to fucking murder you in your fucking tomb when you get here. I swear to Christ you're going to wish for the sun when I'm finished with you."*

"I already do."

About the Author

Kathi Barton, author of the bestselling series Force of Nature, lives in Nashport, Ohio with her husband Paul. In addition to writing full time Kathi likes to spend time with her eight grandkids, three children and three children-in-laws. She writes to relax and have fun.

Her muse, a cross between Jimmy Stewart and Hugh Jackman brings them to life for her readers in a way that has them coming back time and again for more. Her favorite genre is paranormal romance with a great deal of spice. You can visit Kathi on line and drop her an email if you'd like. She loves hearing from her fans. aaronskiss@gmail.com.

Follow Kathi on her blog:
http://kathisbartonauthor.blogspot.com/